Storm Warning...

A brilliant flash of lightning slashed across the night sky. With strong arms, Sam embraced Libby from behind.

"Are you all right?"

"Fine." Libby panted, suddenly flustered by the sound of his husky voice so close to her ear. "Really. And you can let go of me now."

He released her immediately, moving a step backward—or trying to. To Libby's chagrin and considerable discomfort, her single French braid went with him.

"Owww!" she exclaimed.

"Don't move," Sam cautioned, stepping forward quickly. "We're attached."

Now that's an interesting development, Libby thought.

Dear Reader:

Happy holidays! Our authors join me in wishing you all the best for a joyful, loving holiday season with your family and friends. And while celebrating the new year—and the new decade!—I hope you'll think of Silhouette Books.

1990 promises to be especially happy here. This year marks our tenth anniversary, and we're planning a celebration! To symbolize the timelessness of love, as well as the modern gift of the tenth anniversary, each month in 1990, we're presenting readers with a *Diamond Jubilee* Silhouette Romance title, penned by one of your all-time favorite Silhouette Romance authors.

In January, under the Silhouette Romance line's *Diamond Jubilee* emblem, look for Diana Palmer's next book in her bestselling LONG, TALL TEXANS series—*Ethan*. He's a hero sure to lasso your heart! And just in time for Valentine's Day, Brittany Young has written *The Ambassador's Daughter*. Spend the most romantic month of the year in France, the setting for this magical classic. Victoria Glenn, Annette Broadrick, Peggy Webb, Dixie Browning, Phyllis Halldorson—to name just a few!—have written *Diamond Jubilee* titles especially for you. And Pepper Adams has penned a trilogy about three very rugged heroes—and their lovely heroines!—set on the plains of Oklahoma. Look for the first book this summer.

The *Diamond Jubilee* celebration is Silhouette Romance's way of saying thanks to you, our readers. We've been together for ten years now, and with the support you've given us, you can look forward to many more years of heartwarming, poignant love stories.

I hope you'll enjoy this book and all of the stories to come. Come home to romance—Silhouette Romance—for always!

Sincerely,

Tara Hughes Gavin
Senior Editor

LINDA VARNER

Honeymoon Hideaway

Silhouette *Romance*

Published by Silhouette Books New York

America's Publisher of Contemporary Romance

To my husband, Jim,
and our children, Julie and JJ—
the wind beneath my wings

SILHOUETTE BOOKS
300 E. 42nd St., New York, N.Y. 10017

ISBN: 0-373-08698-9

First Silhouette Books printing January 1990

Books by Linda Varner

Silhouette Romance

Heart of the Matter #625
Heart Rustler #644
Luck of the Irish #665
Honeymoon Hideaway #698

LINDA VARNER

has always had a vivid imagination. For that reason, while most people counted sheep to get to sleep, she made up romances. The search for a happy ending sometimes took more than one night, and when one story grew to mammoth proportions, Linda decided to write it down. The result was her first romance novel.

Happily married to her junior high school sweetheart, the mother of two and a full-time secretary, Linda still finds that the best time to plot her latest project is late at night when the house is quiet and she can create without interruption. Linda lives in Conway, Arkansas, where she was raised, and believes the support of her family, friends and writers' group made her dream to be published come true.

ARKANSAS
(YOU RUN DEEP IN ME)
by
Wayland Holyfield

October Morning in the Ozark Mountains
Hills ablazing like that sun in the sky.
I fell in love there and the fire's still burning
A flame that never will die.

Moonlight dancing on the delta levee
To a band of frogs and whippoorwills
I lost my heart there one July evening
And it's still there, I can tell.

Oh, I may wander, but when I do
I will never be far from you.
You're in my blood and I know you'll always be
Arkansas, you run deep in me.

Magnolia blooming, Mam smiling
Mallards sailing on a December wind.
God bless the memories I keep recalling
Like an old familiar friend.

And there's a river rambling through the fields and valleys
Smooth and steady as she makes her way south,
A lot like the people whose name she carries
She goes strong and she goes proud.

Oh, I may wander, but when I do
I will never be far from you.
You're in my blood and I know you'll always be
Arkansas, you run deep in me.

Prologue

*F*ind romance at *Wildwood*

Sam Knight snorted his disgust when he read the words on the picturesque billboard to his right, thinking of the two long days he'd just lost in a Little Rock, Arkansas, divorce court. Romance? Bah, humbug.

He drummed his fingers on the steering wheel of his gleaming black Jaguar, keeping time with the wipers swishing over the rainswept windshield. Impatiently he frowned at the bright red traffic light, willing it to change to green. But it didn't, and his gaze naturally shifted back to that disgusting roadside advertisement, illuminated and shining wetly in the night sky like a beacon for fools.

Specializing in weddings, receptions and first or second honeymoons, he next read, grimacing. Six years' experience as a divorce attorney had long since convinced him that the world would be much better off without honeymoons, not to mention the weddings that preceded them. Belatedly he noticed the other words, almost invisible in the lower right-hand corner of the sign: *Petit Jean Mountain.*

"Aw, hell," Sam groaned, dropping his head downward to rest on the back of his hands. "Not Petit Jean." Why would anyone want to go and deface that beautiful mountain with a honeymoon hotel, of all things? he wondered. And what did that mean to Cedar Ridge Resort, the motel he'd bought there barely a year ago—a fifteen-unit investment that had just begun to make money?

He thought of his rustic resort, bought impulsively after a weekend fishing trip to the central Arkansas mountain where he'd lived as a youngster. He realized it had been over ten months since he'd escaped the confines of his Memphis, Tennessee, law office to visit it and even longer than that since he'd managed to go fishing. Maybe it was time to drive up for a weekend of R and R, he decided, thinking of the solitude of the nearby state park, the comfort of the log fishing cabins, the splendor of the mountain sunrises. He was between court dates. He would borrow a fishing rod, catch a few crappie between rain showers and finally meet the very-capable manager his sister-accountant had hired to run his resort for him.

He would also take a good, long look at this Wildwood place and raise the roof if it compromised, even minutely, the perfection of the mountain he had always considered a haven to the chaos of broken dreams in which he dwelled.

Chapter One

What in the hell have you done to my resort?''

"*Your* resort?" Libby Turner blurted, her automatic smile of welcome vanishing. Her eyes swept the tall stranger who'd just stormed into the lobby of Wildwood—soaked to the skin and leaving in his wake a trail of puddles on her freshly-waxed floor. She took note of short, ash-blond hair plastered to an arrogantly handsome head, wire-rimmed glasses, fogged over and glistening with moisture, and a scowl that brought new meaning to the word *furious*.

"*My* resort," he snapped, snatching off those glasses to reveal eyes as blue as ice ablaze. He yanked a handkerchief from his pocket and applied it to the lenses with an agitated swipe.

"Then you must be—"

"Sam Knight." He shoved the glasses back on.

"What a . . . n-nice surprise," Libby stammered with a hard swallow, immediately on the defensive. This was the first time her long-distance employer had graced Wildwood with his presence since she'd been hired, and from every indication, he wasn't exactly thrilled by the changes she'd made. Why, she couldn't imagine. "I'm Elizabeth Turner, your manager." She extended her hand. He didn't take it. Though irritated by his rudeness, Libby held her own threatening temper in check. He was, after all, very wet— reason enough to be a bear. He was also her boss. Keeping those things firmly in mind, she took her hand back and offered him her brightest smile instead. "It's about time you dropped in to see the miracle we've worked up here."

"Who gave you permission to turn my fishing resort into a honeymoon hotel?" he demanded coldly, his eyes boring into hers. He might as well have said "nuclear waste site." He was that disgusted.

Her jaw dropped in astonishment. "Why, *you* did, of course."

"No, I didn't."

"Yes, you did."

"No, I didn't!" Sam exploded, slapping his flattened palm down on the wooden counter top. Libby jumped nervously in response and took a step back.

"But Ramona told me you loved my idea to turn Cedar Ridge into Wildwood. She said I was to use my own judgment about decor and—"

"Ramona, huh?" Sam brusquely interjected, "I should have known. Where's your telephone? I'm going to call that sister of mine right now and get to the bottom of this."

He reached for the phone, but Libby was too quick for him, covering the instrument with her hand. "Are you telling me you didn't know what was going on up here?" she demanded, eyes wide.

"That's exactly what I'm telling you," he replied, peeling her fingers from the telephone and wrapping his own around the receiver.

"But you paid for it," she argued, clamping both her hands on top of his.

He glared at her. "I paid for 'major renovations' that the 'new manager'—" his accusing gaze raked her "—had recommended to turn Cedar Ridge into a money-making investment. Ramona took care of all the details, and she never said anything about any honeymoon hotel—probably because she knew I would nix the idea."

"But why? Arkansas *needs* a honeymoon hideaway like this."

He laughed shortly. "Like it needs another politician. You're talking to a divorce lawyer, Ms, Turner. Romance, love and happily-ever-afters are myths that I want no part in perpetrating." With his free hand, he pried her fingers off of his.

Libby grabbed the whole phone then, scooping it up and hugging it to her chest, arms crossed protectively over it. "How can you say such a thing?" she demanded hotly. "Love is no myth."

"Tell that to the man I represented in court today," Sam said. "The woman who swore undying devotion barely a year ago just sued him for his house, his car, his kid *and* sixty-five percent of his yearly income."

Libby winced at his harsh words. "That's an isolated case."

"Isolated, hell. Shall I quote the divorce statistics?"

"Please don't," she murmured, well aware of those statistics and doing her best to change them.

"Good. Then you undoubtedly understand why I might be a little upset that the two of you went behind my back and—"

"I did *not* go behind your back! I never dreamed Ramona hadn't told you the truth."

Sam digested her heated words in silence, his face stony. "Are you willing to let me check out your story with my sister?"

"Of course, I am," Libby said, bristling at his obvious doubt.

"Then give me the phone!"

She did, slamming it down on the counter with a vengeance, a crash and a jangle. While Sam punched out the number, Libby put some distance between them, stomping away to stand by the door that led to a hallway and her living quarters. She paused there, breathing deeply in an attempt to gain control of her temper. She didn't like Sam Knight—couldn't believe this pessimistic grump was related to a hopeful romantic like Ramona Wilson.

Physically, of course, the siblings had much in common: Paul Newman-blue eyes, straight nose, high cheekbones. There the resemblance ended, however. Sam's chiseled jawline, firm lips and muscular build were strictly masculine, and the set of his chin hinted at a ruthlessness his easygoing sister definitely didn't share. Libby couldn't help but wonder if his face would crack if he smiled, and decided she would probably never find out.

At that moment, the object of her inspection dropped the receiver back into its cradle. His steely stare found and locked with Libby's, leaving her more than a little flustered. Determined not to let him intimidate her further, she stuffed her fingertips into the pockets of her jeans and squared her shoulders, staring right back at him. "No answer? Well, it *is* Friday night and early yet. Don't she and Thomas usually take in a movie on their way home?"

"Oh, yeah," he muttered sheepishly, shoulders sagging. Then he frowned at her. "How'd you know that?"

"She and I are good friends—have been since high school," Libby told him with a shrug.

"I didn't realize..." Sam's words trailed off into silence, and he studied her intently, clearly trying to remember her from his youth. Libby knew he wouldn't have any luck. He was at least nine or ten years older than her own twenty-seven and had already been away at law school when she and Ramona were still giggling teenagers.

"It's true, and I met her husband, Thomas, for the first time when they came up here for their wedding last month."

Sam grimaced. "So this is where they got off to. Somehow that doesn't surprise me. Those starry-eyed lovebirds probably *would* enjoy hot-pink love tubs, genuine polyester bearskin rugs and heart-shaped waterbeds."

Libby gasped at the insult and lost the temper she'd managed to hold in check thus far. "How dare you say such a thing about my motel! This is the very first time you've been by since I've remodeled, and you haven't even seen the rooms yet."

"This is *my* motel," Sam retorted, eyes narrowed. "And if I'd had any idea what you and Ramona were up to, I'd have been up here in a New York minute to stop you. As it is, I'm here now and since my car is buried up in that ditch back at the turn off, I—"

"You had a *wreck*?" Libby blurted in horror, cutting off the rest of his tirade. Her anger suddenly replaced by concern for an old friend's only brother, she hurried back over to Sam to worriedly peruse his flushed face. "Why didn't you say something, for Pete's sake? Are you all right?"

"I just ditched my car and hiked half a mile in a typhoon to discover that my ditzy sister and a manager I'd never met have changed my fishing resort into a honeymoon hotel *without even consulting me.* Do I sound 'all right' to you?"

Libby gulped audibly and flew around the end of the counter to catch hold of his arm. Urgently she pulled on it, trying to coax him the two short steps to the couch. "You sit down right here. I'm calling an ambulance." Keeping a hand on his biceps, she reached back for the phone, but he was too quick for her, sabotaging the effort by grabbing the instrument with both hands—a technique he'd probably just learned.

"I have a better idea," he said, his face now millimeters from hers. "Why don't you just give me a room instead? I'd like to get out of these wet clothes before I try to call my sister again. Then I need to get hold of a twenty-four-hour wrecker service somewhere."

"You want a room?" Libby squeaked, her stomach suddenly knotting.

"I want a room."

"Here?"

"Of course, here."

Libby cleared her throat and braced herself. "I can't give you one."

"Why not?" he demanded predictably. Then his eyes glittered with suspicion. "Afraid I won't like what I see, after all?"

"On the contrary, Mr. Knight," she retorted, bristling once more. "I'd be proud to put you up at Wildwood tonight. Unfortunately, there aren't any vacancies."

He gaped at her. "You can't be serious. It's October. The tourist season is long over."

"Romance knows no season," Libby reminded him, adding, "Our rooms are booked solid until after Valentine's Day."

"I don't believe it."

"You'd better. Wildwood is *the* place to honeymoon these days. Didn't you read this month's issue of *Nuptials*?

"No, I did not read this month's issue of *Nuptials*," he retorted.

"Too bad," she told him, unable to hide her smug smile. "We got a five-star rating, both on accommodations and locale. You should be proud to be the owner of such a successful establishment."

"Proud, hell." He dropped abruptly down onto the couch and leaned back, closing his eyes. Libby noted that the color had drained from his cheeks. Really concerned now, she sat down on the edge of the cushion beside him.

"Are you sure you're not hurt?"

"Positive," he replied without opening his eyes. Libby didn't believe him.

"Look," she ventured, suddenly remorseful. "Why don't you sleep in my bed tonight?" When his eyes flew open at her thoughtless question, she blushed, hastily adding, "I'll drive to my mother's when I get off at midnight."

"Where does your mother live?" Sam asked, obviously weighing the merits of her plan.

"Morrilton."

"Forget it," he murmured immediately, leaning forward to prop his elbows on his knees. "That's twenty miles of winding roads. I know from experience that they're wet and slick tonight."

"I've done it hundreds of times," Libby airily assured him, getting to her feet. "I'll be fine. Now you just sit tight. I'll have everything ready for you in a minute." She managed one step away before Sam caught her hand in his and halted her.

"I said, forget it," he repeated, his authoritative tone brooking no argument.

"You have a better plan?" Libby countered, tugging her fingers free of his and glaring at him.

Sam looked down at the couch on which he sat. "Maybe. Does this become a bed?"

Libby shook her head.

"Then I guess I'll have to go to Mather Lodge over in the state park."

"They're full up, too. One of the local churches is having a retreat this weekend."

Sam sighed heavily. "Are you positive you don't have just one empty cabin tucked away somewhere?"

"Of course, I'm positive, unless you count Fetch's house, out back."

"Fetch?"

"My Labrador retriever."

"He doesn't sleep there?"

"He sleeps with me."

Sam's gaze swept Libby from head to toe. Lucky dog, he thought, immediately wondering where *that* errant thought had come from. Though rather pretty, with a face and figure a connoisseur like Sam could well appreciate, Libby Turner was nonetheless not his type. Worse, she was in cahoots with his sister. "What about that old cabin across the lake? Is it still there?"

"It is, and it's rented," she replied.

Frantically Sam searched for a solution to his dilemma. It wasn't easy. After the events of the past few hours, he felt brain dead. "What about a rollaway bed? Surely you have one of those."

"I have three brand-new ones," Libby responded, visibly brightening. "They're stored in unit six right now."

Sam arched an eyebrow. "Unit six isn't rented out?"

"No. It's under repair. Three weeks ago lightning split that old oak tree beside it, and the part that broke off tore up the roof and shattered a window. I had major water damage inside and probably won't be able to reopen it until sometime next week."

"Is the place sleepable?" Sam then asked, that elusive idea he'd been seeking finally making its appearance.

"I suppose so," Libby replied with a little shrug. "The roof is repaired, and there are lights and running water. The new carpet hasn't been laid yet, though, or the curtains hung, and there's a sheet of plastic instead of glass on the window. It may be warm now, but you'll freeze once the cold front that's causing all these thunderstorms finally gets here."

"That's not supposed to be until late tomorrow, and you've got blankets, haven't you?" he asked, getting to his feet.

"Well, yes..." She paused, frowning. "It just doesn't seem right for you to rough it in your own resort. *I'll* sleep in unit six. You can have my apartment."

"No, I'll be fine."

Libby opened her mouth, fully intending, he suspected, to argue. However, she obviously thought better of that and shut it again. "Then you'll need sheets, a pillow, towels, washcloths and extra blankets."

Sam nodded his agreement, relieved Libby wasn't going to give him any static after all. Suddenly wiped out, no doubt in reaction to his close encounter with the ditch, Sam wasn't sure he was up to it at the moment. Sitting back down on the couch to wait, he watched Libby cross the room and disappear through an open door.

Unconsciously, he approved of the view from that side as much as he had the other *and* in spite of his earlier decision that she wasn't his type. She was a striking woman for all her foolish notions about love and romance—taller than average, with a slender build and delicate bone structure that belied the fire in her big brown eyes. The tendrils of dark brown hair that framed her oval face did nothing to dispel the air of fragility surrounding her, an air Sam suspected might be a tad deceptive. He was sure of it when she returned moments later, peeking over the huge stack of linens she clutched as she made her way to the exit.

"Do you need some help?" he asked.

"You can be in charge of your key," she told him, holding her bundle secure with her chin while she tossed the key to him. "I can manage the rest." Sam pocketed the key when he caught it and moved to follow her. When they got to the door, he reached around her, pushing on the heavy glass so she could step out onto the porch.

"Watch my bag there on your left," Sam cautioned. "I left it out here a while ago."

"Thanks," Libby replied, noting with relief that the steady rain that had poured all day had slowed to a sprinkle for the moment. Just as the door shut behind them, a brilliant flash of lightning slashed across the night sky. Libby gasped and stopped short, an action that sent Sam, who was right on her heels, careening into her. She stumbled into his leather carryall, bobbling her load as she fought for balance and scattering towels, wash cloths and sheets in every direction.

Sam engulfed Libby with strong arms from behind, saving both her and the remains of her burden from a similar fate. Before she could free herself, thunder crashed. The porch beneath their feet shuddered with the force of the sound, and Libby tensed in fear. It was all she could do not to toss aside the blankets and pillow she still held and turn to bury her face in the broad chest of the man behind her.

"Are you all right?"

"Fine," Libby panted, suddenly as flustered by the sound of his husky voice, so close to her ear, as she was by the dancing lightning. "Really. And you can let go of me now."

He released her immediately, moving a step backward—or trying to. To Libby's chagrin, and considerable discomfort, her single French braid went with him.

"Ow!" she exclaimed, helpless to reach behind her head to see what was wrong.

"Don't move," Sam cautioned, stepping quickly forward again. "We're attached."

Now that's an interesting development, Libby thought, disgustingly aware of his lean body pressed to hers. She tried to turn her head to see what had happened.

"Don't move," he repeated sternly.

Libby felt Sam's hands working the braid—his fingers brushing against the back of her neck, which positively tingled with embarrassment. Though a brunette like her mother, Libby had nonetheless inherited some of her red-headed father's coloring, namely his freckles and easy blush response. She'd also gotten her fair share of his short temper, a fact she had already rued more than once since Sam Knight had burst into her life.

It seemed as though an eternity passed before Sam grunted in satisfaction and freed her, explaining, "My button got caught in your hair."

She turned to face him then, noting with a start that he had actually managed a smile of sorts, an expression that hadn't cracked his face at all, but sent a breathtaking twinkle to those baby blues of his. Libby's heart did a backflip in response, and she acknowledged that the man was more than good looking. He was some kind of gorgeous. And his proximity was about to get the best of her. How odd, she mused. She'd been around handsome men before, and this one wasn't even her type. Rattled, Libby knelt to gather her scattered load.

"Doesn't look like anything got wet," Sam commented, bending down to help her.

"No, it doesn't," she agreed, marveling that he could carry on such a normal conversation. She found she could still barely breathe, and every inhalation she *did* manage was laced with the scent of his musky after-shave. Her next words came out an octave higher than usual. "I think it might be wise if I went and got a plastic bag to put them in, though."

Sam frowned, no doubt noting her agitation. "Sure you're okay?"

"I'm sure," she said. "Ever since lightning struck our tree, I've been jumpy as all get out every time it storms."

"I can imagine," he murmured.

Haphazardly, Libby restacked her load and got to her feet. Then she retreated to her cabin, returning moments later with a large plastic bag that she stuffed full of the bed clothes.

Sam reached out and took the bundle, cutting off her immediate objection with a firm, "I'll carry that. You get my bag. It's not heavy."

She didn't argue. As they moved for the steps, Libby heard the sudden rush of wind through the dense woods surrounding them and realized a wall of rain was fast approaching. She caught Sam's arm, stopping him.

"It's not far, but I'd better drive you there anyway."

When he nodded his agreement, Libby led the way down the two steps to the motel's van. But the back doors of the vehicle were locked tight, and too late Libby realized that she should have located her keys before she and Sam left the protection of the porch. As the rain began to fall in earnest, Libby frantically patted each and every pocket of her khaki pants, her heart sinking when she failed to locate the keys.

Belatedly remembering where they were, she scurried around the van to open the side door, yanking the elusive ring from the ignition. At that moment, the sky opened up, drenching both her and her already-saturated guest. Hastily, she rounded the van to jam the keys in the lock and throw open the double doors. Sam tossed both bags inside and slammed the doors.

"Can you swim?" Libby yelled over the roar of the rain in the feeble hope that Sam might see the humor of their situation. She wasn't really surprised when he didn't, instead reaching out to grasp her arm and propel her firmly to the front of the van. There he opened the door and handed her up behind the steering wheel. Seconds later, he got into the other seat. Libby snapped herself out of her daze of embarrassment with difficulty and stuck the key in the ignition.

She could just imagine what her employer must think of her performance thus far. It was bad enough that he believed she was in on Ramona's deception. Now he probably wondered if she had the brains to run his motel in the first place. Quickly, Libby started the engine, turned on the lights and put the van in motion, turning it sharply down the narrow graveled drive that led to unit six, a few yards to the north. When the sweeping headlights illuminated some of the results of her recent handiwork, she smiled to herself.

Wildwood was beautiful—a dream come true for Libby, who had first hatched the idea of bringing a honeymoon resort to Arkansas while still a homesick student at the University of Nevada, getting her degree in hotel management. She was proud of what she'd accomplished in her ten short months at Petit Jean. Nestled in a dense forest high atop the beautiful mountain, this rustic resort for married couples provided a haven of seclusion from the stresses modern-day living could put on any union. Accommodations ranged from reasonably priced units with kitchenettes to plush honeymoon suites, all housed in picturesque log cabins. On top of that, Wildwood boasted a chapel, a new swimming pool, a restaurant large enough to serve as a reception hall and a sauna. There was also a small lake complete with an island gazebo and both fishing and paddle boats and, for those not into water sports, a tennis court.

There was no way Sam could view all this splendor and doubt her managerial abilities, she decided. But one glance in his direction told her he was paying no attention at all to the beauty around him. Obviously exhausted, he'd closed his eyes and tipped his head back to make use of the head-rest. Though tempted to point out this and that change, she wisely kept her mouth shut. He looked to be in no mood for the grand tour just yet, and she didn't want to do anything to anger him further.

Tomorrow would be soon enough to show him around the place. Meanwhile, it might be wise to do everything she possibly could to make Sam Knight's stay perfect from this moment on. But how could everything be perfect? His cabin wasn't near ready for occupation. The bed wasn't made, and the rest of the furniture was stacked and covered with plastic sheeting. There weren't even any drapes....

Libby realized with dismay that she had a heck of a lot to do before she could properly welcome her guest. Welcome her guest? Libby sighed heavily, acknowledging that was the least of her worries this night. First and foremost was the formidable task of salvaging her reputation as a manager and convincing Sam that she was an innocent party to Ramona's deception.

That determined, Libby turned the van between two trees, halting it as close as she could to the cabin where Sam would sleep that night. They both got out of the vehicle, Sam waving her on to shelter. By the time he unloaded and stepped onto the porch with the linens and bag, Libby had opened the door and flipped on the lights. Sam stood in silence when he entered the stuffy cabin, turning slowly to peruse every inch of the cluttered living room.

Most of the furniture had been pushed to the middle of the floor and covered with a dropcloth. There were paint cans everywhere, not to mention pop bottles, variously shaped styrofoam containers and candy wrappers left by the numerous workers who'd eaten there during the process of repair the past week. The concrete floor beneath their feet—plainly visible since the carpet hadn't been relaid yet—was littered with sawdust, bits of wood and stray nails.

Libby, seeing the area through his eyes, didn't know whether to laugh or cry. She glanced at her guest, whose expression revealed nothing of his thoughts. "Why don't you have a seat somewhere while I set things to rights?"

"Why bother for one night?" he asked, pinching the muscles at the base of his neck with a thumb and forefinger. "I'm really beat, and there's the little matter of these wet clothes. All I need is one of those beds and a telephone."

"Right," Libby responded briskly. She dumped her load on one of the shrouded chairs and crossed over to a window, raising it to let in some fresh air. Then she walked to the corner of the room and the rollaway beds she'd recently purchased—beds she would have to store somewhere else once this cabin was fully functional again. Sam helped her maneuver one of the folded-up beds to the center of the room, where they opened it with a twist of the screws.

Libby then retrieved the sheets, hastily making the bed and piling the extra blankets at the foot of it. She wished she could offer Sam better sleeping accommodations, but knew that this thin mattress was the best she could do for now.

"Sure you want to sleep here?" she asked, giving him one last chance to change his mind.

"Positive," he assured her.

Shrugging in resignation, she showed him the phone, closet, bathroom and kitchenette before she moved toward the door, turning to face him again when she reached it. "If you think of anything else you need, I'm just a yell away."

"Thanks," he replied, joining her there.

For some reason, Libby suddenly felt reluctant to leave. She suspected it was because Sam looked so dead on his feet. Once again she wondered if he were really as well as he claimed to be. "Promise you're okay?"

"Yes." His answer was clipped, dismissive.

She took the hint. "Then I'd better get back to work. It was very nice to meet you, Mr. Knight." Impulsively she extended her right hand.

Taken aback by her unexpected formality, Sam nonetheless took her slender hand in his, shaking it. "You may as well call me Sam."

Her brilliant smile brought to life two perfect dimples and made Sam's heart skip a beat. "If you'll call me Libby." When he nodded, she stepped out the door. "Good night . . . Sam."

"Good night," he replied.

Libby didn't bother with the steps, instead jumping off the porch to splash her way to the van. She got in and shut her door, pulling away with a crunch of mud and gravel.

Lost in thought, Sam shut his door, too. What a day, he mused as he opened his bag and dug out the well-worn sweats he loved. Then he rummaged around for underwear, thankful his housekeeper, Ava, had packed extras, as usual. More than once an out-of-state court case had dragged on longer than anticipated, and the clean clothes had come in handy. And, though it was pleasure instead of business that kept him in Arkansas over the weekend, Ava's foresight was much appreciated.

Pleasure? Sam frowned as he headed for the privacy of the bathroom, clothes in hand. Hardly pleasure—at least now that Ramona had pulled her latest fast one. And what a fast one she'd pulled this time! He couldn't imagine what had motivated her to such deceitfulness. Or could he?

While stripping off his drenched clothes and draping them neatly over the curtain rod of the not-so-clean shower, Sam realized his younger sister just might have reason to try to make his life miserable after all. Up until a month ago, he'd certainly been doing his level best to do the same for her.

He'd had good reason at the time, of course. Ramona had gone and gotten herself engaged to a divorcé with children, of all people. Sam's experience in divorce court told him their marriage had about as much chance for survival as a turkey at Thanksgiving. As a result, he'd done his damnedest to talk her out of what would surely prove to be the biggest mistake of her life...but to no avail, since Ramona was as hardheaded as she was hopelessly romantic. Sam could only hope the wedded bliss they now claimed would last, even though he seriously doubted it.

Sam dried his lean body on one of the towels Libby had left him before stepping into dry undershorts and the tattered sweats. He looked into the mirror over the sink as he combed his wet hair, grimacing at the weary man who stared back at him. Seconds later found him sitting on the narrow bed, telephone in hand.

He had no better luck reaching Ramona this time and put the instrument aside with disgust. Tomorrow he would reach her, he silently vowed. And tomorrow he would give her orders to sell Wildwood to one of the two motel chains that had made offers on his resort in the last couple of weeks—offers that had surprised him at the time, but now made perfect sense.

Thinking back to Ramona's clever handling of said offers made him realize just how easily he'd been manipulated by her. She'd presented each in a negative way, and, distracted as usual by his work, Sam had given her only half his attention before telling her to do whatever she thought best. Obviously he'd given his sister far too much leeway in her capacity as his money manager and would now have to pay for his lack of judgment. He could only hope his law partners didn't learn about this motel monkey business. They would never let him forget it.

Sam looked around the room for a telephone book, fully intending to locate and call a wrecker service. There was no book, however, and grumbling to himself, he abandoned that effort until tomorrow, too. It was highly unlikely that anyone would bother his car on a night like this even if they found it, which they probably never would as it was definitely off the beaten path.

So what now? he asked himself, glancing around the depressingly empty room. Though physically exhausted, he was much too wired to fall asleep just yet. He wished for his briefcase, a television or a radio, none of which were available, and abruptly realized his tumultuous thoughts were the only company he would have until dawn. And what thoughts. Trying not to dwell on how easily he'd been duped by little sis over the past few months, Sam searched for something else—anything else—to think about. Not surprisingly, a vision of Libby popped into his head—Libby with eyes so dark he couldn't even see the pupils, Libby in a waterlogged T-shirt and pants that clung to every feminine curve....

Sam groaned loudly when he realized what direction his thoughts had taken, and he plopped back on the bed, sternly reminding himself that this same Libby had also joined forces with his sister and was going to lose her job as a result of her indiscretion. Not that he intended to fire her right away. He wouldn't . . . at least not until he knew the whole truth and then with reluctance, since she was clearly very bright.

But Libby's future was not his problem, and, after he talked to Ramona tomorrow, Wildwood wouldn't be, either...thank God.

The rain finally stopped a couple of hours later, and shortly after that Gil Turner, Libby's older brother, showed up for his usual weeknight twelve-to-eight desk duty. After a brief explanation about the surprise guest in unit six, Libby walked back to her living quarters and Fetch, her two-year-old dog. He greeted her with a yelp of delight and a very cold nose, which he nuzzled into her palm.

After placing a kiss on his velvety black head, Libby made tracks to the refrigerator for her usual late night cola. Then, canned soft drink in hand, she stepped out the back door onto her darkened porch and the bench swing both she and Fetch adored. She steadied the swing so Fetch could jump up on it, joining him there a second later. He loved to swing; she loved to star gaze. They'd passed many a companionable, late-night hour there on the recesses of the porch, now thrown into deep shadow by the nearby security light that illuminated the immediate area.

Libby reached out, absently petting Fetch, who took that gesture as an invitation to crawl in her lap. Since he weighed a good eighty pounds, she laughingly pushed him away.

"Sorry, sport," she said, steadying the swing. Fetch yawned his disappointment and lay back down. Really relaxing for the first time that night, Libby set the swing in motion and glanced skyward, observing with pleasure the single star that twinkled through a fleeting break in the dense clouds overhead. She made a wish and then laughed at her foolishness. Wishes only came true in fairy tales, and Fetch might not appreciate being turned into a knight in shining armor.

Knight? Libby glanced automatically toward the cabin down the trail, noting that that particular Knight's light still burned. Apparently he was a night owl, too, or maybe he was still trying to get hold of Ramona.

And what would he say to her once he reached her? Libby wondered, glad she wasn't Sam's younger sister tonight. Not that Ramona didn't deserve whatever punishment he dished out. As far as Libby was concerned, she certainly did. Her duplicity was unforgiveable and . . . baffling.

Why *had* Ramona tricked her brother? Because he was so dead set against marriage and she knew he would veto their renovation plans? Undoubtedly, Libby decided, next wondering why Sam was so against marriage and honeymoons in the first place. Was his occupation solely to blame? Or something else?

Lost in her musing, Libby sipped her soft drink. At that moment, Fetch tensed beside her. She automatically followed the direction of her pet's gaze to Sam's lighted cabin, noting that her guest now stood square in front of the open window, his back to her. Shirtless, he was a sight to behold, and Libby halted the motion of the swing, leaning forward for a better view. Her appreciative gaze missed not one golden-bronzed inch of his broad back, narrow waist and powerful arms.

Fetch, no doubt wondering why the rhythmic movement he loved had suddenly ceased, sharply barked his complaint, Libby panicked, clamping her fingers over his muzzle to hush him. She told herself that though Sam had turned toward the sound and now stared out the window, he couldn't really see her huddling there in the dark like some Peeping Tom.

Or could he? She held her breath.

Sam stood motionless for several seconds and then disappeared from view. A heartbeat later, his front door flew open, an action that sent Libby bounding off the swing and into the cover of her cabin.

Chapter Two

Bright sunlight woke Libby the next morning—sunlight streaming through the window of her bedroom-living room combination in the log cabin that housed her living quarters, the restaurant and the office of Wildwood. She rolled over to avoid the glare, not an easy task since Fetch lay sprawled across her legs, and risked a quick peek at the alarm clock before smiling and snuggling farther under the covers.

Nine o'clock on a Saturday. That meant that Charlotte, the cousin who worked weekends, had relieved Gil on the desk an hour ago. All was right at Wildwood; Libby could sleep until noon if she pleased.

"Jumping Jehoshaphat!" she exclaimed barely two seconds later, sitting bolt upright in bed and struggling to extract her legs from under her sleeping canine. "Will you move it? I've got to get in gear. I promised Charlotte I'd work for her this morning!"

With difficulty, Libby tossed back the quilt and wiggled free to scramble off the bed. She threw off her cotton sleep shirt as she dashed to the bathroom and, in seconds, stood in front of the sink dressed in pale pink undies, splashing cold water on her sleepy eyes. Two swipes of the hairbrush later, Libby tugged on the blue jeans, a white sweatshirt boldly airbrushed with the logo of Dogpatch USA and well-worn penny loafers.

Promising herself she would slip away from the desk first chance she got to do a better job of her toilette, Libby then charged out the door and down the short hallway to the lobby.

"Why didn't you wake me?" she demanded of her brother as she burst into the room, Fetch on her heels.

But it wasn't her brother who swiveled his stool around to face her. It was Sam Knight, sitting behind the check-in desk with a telephone receiver to each ear.

"It's about time," he grumbled, tossing one of them to her. "I finally got Ramona. She wants to talk to you."

As a stunned Libby bobbled and then caught the instrument, Sam turned his attention back to the red in-house phone. Since Gil was nowhere to be seen, Libby quickly surmised that Sam had relieved him on the desk. She couldn't imagine why, but it was obvious her brother had briefed their guest on procedure before he left. Sam, a note pad and oversize menu laid out before him, appeared well prepared to take and forward to the restaurant the breakfast requests that always poured in that time of day.

Assured that the situation was well in hand—at least for the moment—Libby stretched the extra-long telephone cord to its limit and stepped back out into the hall, pushing the door as near closed as she could.

"Good morning," she said sweetly, once she'd put the receiver to her ear. "And how are you today?"

"How am *I*?" Ramona Wilson squawked. "How are *you*?"

"Just dandy considering I'm now an accomplice to what could well be the scam of the century."

"Oh, Lord, I'm sorry. Was Sam very upset?"

"You could say that," Libby told her with remarkable calm.

"Then we're even, because I've been mad as hops at him ever since he bought Cedar Ridge Resort and dumped it on me."

"Is that why you lied to him—to get even for all the extra work?"

"I never actually lied," Ramona said. "And just between you and me, this renovation project hasn't been work at all. I've had a ball."

"Don't you feel the least bit guilty about tricking him?"

"Of course not. I had to do it. Why, he'd never have agreed to the wonderful changes you suggested. Besides, he deserved a little misery for being such a jerk about my engagement to Thomas."

"That's no excuse for being so...so..." Libby fumbled in vain for a word to justly describe her friend's actions.

"Sneaky?" Ramona offered with a giggle.

"This isn't funny!" Libby snapped. Then she sighed, immediately regretting her sharp tone. There was no sense in losing her temper now. The harm had already been done. "Sorry. I'm a little uptight this morning."

"And no wonder, with my Scrooge of a brother breathing down your neck," Ramona replied. "But you can relax. I've already confessed and convinced Sam that you're innocent. He's promised to give you a good reference when he sells Wildwood."

"*Sells* Wildwood? After all that work?" Libby screeched, immediately clamping her hand over her mouth. She eased the door back open a scant inch so she could peek out at Sam, who sat with his back to her, still busy with the phone. Letting out her pent-up breath, she shut the door again and leaned against the wall for support. "He can't."

"Wanna bet? We've already had two offers on the place."

"Oh, no," Libby groaned, sliding weakly down the wall to sit on her heels. "Who made them?" Her heart sank when Ramona named two well-established, well-to-do franchises. "But Wildwood will be just another motel if he sells to either of them. Besides, they only hire graduates of their own training programs. I'll lose my job."

"Not if you play your cards right," Ramona smoothly responded. "And that's why I need to talk to you."

"What are you up to now?" Libby asked, suddenly flooded with memories of their high school days and a few other crazy schemes in which she'd been an unwitting, unwilling participant.

"Just this. Sam told me about his head-on with the ditch last night. Apparently he's already called a mechanic and found out that the nearest repair shop is only open until noon today and not at all on Sunday. That means you've got him until Monday, anyway."

"But I don't want him until Monday," Libby wailed.

"Sure you do," Ramona argued. "It'll take that long, at least, for you to persuade him not to sell out."

"And how on earth am I supposed to do that?"

"Easy. All you have to do is convince him that a hideaway like Wildwood puts the romance in a marriage and that romance is necessary to keep love alive and a couple together."

"You call that *easy*?" Clearly Ramona had finally plunged over the edge of sanity. Libby knew from experience how easy it would be to tumble after her.

"I certainly do. You two *are* at a honeymoon retreat, aren't you?"

"You know we are."

"Then you merely show Sam all the happy couples milling about. Once he realizes there's more to life than divorce court, the rest will be a snap."

"Ramona...dearest," Libby said through gritted teeth. "You're forgetting one little detail."

"What's that?"

"The couples who come to Wildwood do not mill about. They have better things to do...indoors."

"Oops. Good point," Ramona said, giggling again as she added, "Well, you still have Plan B."

"Which is?" Libby prompted, not in the least surprised that a Plan B existed.

"Seduce my brother."

"What!"

"Now don't blow a gasket," Ramona cautioned. "Sam's really not so bad once you get to know him, and he's darned good looking, if I do say so. Unfortunately, he's lost his perspective—forgotten how wonderful it is to be in love."

"He's been in love?" Libby blurted, distracted for the moment from the ludicrousness of Plan B.

"In love and married, though he isn't either one anymore. Sam seldom dates these days and swears he's happy living like a monk. Frankly, I don't believe him. He's lonely, and I figure a little female attention is all it will take to remind him how much fun romance can be."

"Well, you're going to have to find yourself another female to do the dirty work," Libby told her with a decisive nod. "I'm not the seducing kind, and even if I were, I would never pick your big brother as my prey. We didn't exactly hit it off last night."

"That was last night. Now that he knows you're innocent, things will be different."

"Bull. He's a hopeless realist; I'm a hopeful romantic. And contrary to popular belief, opposites do not attract. Plan B is absolutely out of the question."

"But think what's at stake—"

"No!"

A long silence followed Libby's vehement refusal. Then Ramona heaved a sigh of resignation. "I suppose you're right. Even *your* sunny smile couldn't melt that Arctic winter heart of his."

"For once we agree on something," Libby murmured, relieved she wasn't going to have to argue with her headstrong friend. "So why don't we move on to Plan C?"

"Because there isn't one," Ramona admitted, adding, "Not yet, anyway. Surely between the two of us, we can come up with something."

"Surely. And let's keep it clean, shall we? I have some scruples, even if you don't."

"Right," Ramona agreed with a low laugh that made Libby's stomach knot in dread. "Now you call me if you think of anything, and I'll do the same, okay?"

"Okay. Bye, Mona."

"Bye."

Libby stood in silence for a moment after the bubbly blonde got off the line, thinking about their incredible conversation. She shook her head in disbelief as she reached for the doorknob and then laughed softly to herself. Seduce Sam Knight, indeed. Imagine Ramona even suggesting such a thing.

Bemused, Libby opened the door to the office. She stepped inside, halting abruptly when she saw that Fetch had made friends with the boss and now lay sprawled at his feet, chin resting on one of Sam's leather deck shoes. Of it's own volition, Libby's gaze inched upward the length of Sam's denim-clad leg to the maroon cotton sweater that hugged wide shoulders and accentuated a well-muscled neck.

Seduce Sam Knight? *Indeed.*

As if you could. Libby immediately scolded herself, getting a grip on her errant thoughts with effort. Monk or hunk, Sam Knight was more man than she had ever encountered, and it would take more woman than Libby Turner to seduce him. Assuming she wanted to. Which she didn't. That reaffirmed, she walked on into the room, greeting her pet, a sound that made Sam swivel to face her once more. With a sigh of relief, he stepped clear of the ebony canine and stood.

"I think I got all the orders down right, but I haven't had a chance to call the restaurant."

"I'll take care of it," she said, slipping past him to hang up the phone before she took her place on the stool, still warm from his body heat. "Have you eaten?"

"Not yet."

"Why don't you go get yourself a bite of breakfast next door? My mother is the cook, and the food is wonderful."

"All right." He turned as though to leave, but hesitated. "It seems I owe you an apology."

"Oh?"

"Yes. I'm, uh, sorry about last night, and just for the record, I consider this hour at the desk just penance for my sins."

Libby couldn't help but laugh at his words, knowing how hectic the weekend morning shift could be. "More than just, I expect."

Once again Sam turned toward the door. Once again, he halted. "I talked to a mechanic a while ago, a man named George Cardin in Morrilton."

"George is a first cousin of mine," Libby said.

"Really? Well, he told me it would be Monday before he could get to my car, but he promised to send someone after it around eleven this morning. I thought I'd hitch a ride in with the wrecker so I can talk to him in person...if you think you can send someone after me, that is."

"I'll come get you myself," Libby assured him. "I have an errand to run in town when I get off at noon, anyway."

Sam nodded in reply and pushed open the door that connected the office to the restaurant. A second later, Libby found herself alone with a ringing house phone. Humming softly, a satisfied smile on her face, she settled herself more comfortably on the stool and picked up the phone. "Front desk. May I help you?"

It was almost two hours later before Libby found a minute to herself again. She used that minute to wave a goodbye to Sam, now headed down the narrow asphalt road to wait for the wrecker. Though Libby would have loved to abandon her post to watch the rescue of his car, she didn't dare. Check-out time was fast approaching, and several new guests were expected to arrive shortly after that. She had plenty to keep her occupied until her teenaged cousin Katrina arrived to relieve her.

Libby had several cousins whom she employed at Wildwood—both full-time and part-time. The resort also provided a means of income for her aunt, who owned a cleaning business, and, of course, her mom and brother. Her dad often helped out in a pinch, fixing anything that broke down, supplementing the money he earned at his appliance repair shop.

For that reason, Sam's decision to sell Wildwood weighed heavily on Libby's mind the rest of the morning. By the time Katrina bounced into the office at noon, all smiles and brimming with plans for the paycheck awaiting her, Libby knew for a certainty she had to come up with a Plan C...and pronto.

But what could it be? Obviously mere arguments would never convince Sam of the merits of a honeymoon resort. Divorce lawyer that he was, he'd always have a rebuttal. Gloomily, Libby searched her brain for another idea. She found none, however, and by the time she finished briefing Katrina and headed back to her apartment to freshen up, Ramona's seduction idea had begun to have a certain amount of appeal.

Ramona should know him better than anyone, Libby rationalized as she slipped out of her clothes. And Ramona believed that a little romance would do wonders for his disposition. Dyed-in-the-wool romantic Libby never questioned that logic for a minute. She did question the choice of seductress, however, since she had no intentions of getting involved with Sam Knight in any way except professionally.

Pulling on a navy-blue tank top, a bright yellow blouse, which she left unbuttoned and tied at her waist, and pleated khaki pants, Libby made mental inventory of the other available females in the area. She focused her search on relatives, in particular her innumerable cousins and aunts. Unfortunately, most of them were married, a fact Libby's parents pointed out to her every time she served as bridesmaid.

She had a stock answer to their not-so-subtle hints that it was high time to be the bride, assuring them that she fully intended to be...the moment her long-awaited knight rushed in on his white steed to sweep her off her feet and into his loving arms. Meanwhile she bided her time, directed her romantic energies into Wildwood and lived vicariously each and every happily-ever-after she witnessed.

Libby plopped down on the bed so she could slip on a pair of flats. A second later found her in the bathroom, brushing her hair as she continued to search her brain for a female qualified to remind Sam how marvelous romance could be. Only one came to mind, mechanic George Cardin's divorced daughter, Patty. A shameless flirt, Patty was everything Libby wasn't—petite, beautiful, chic. Libby had no doubt that young woman would welcome a chance at a male as influential as Sam. Whether or not Patty actually succeeded in *seducing* him really didn't matter as long as he experienced a change of heart. In fact, Libby half hoped they would share nothing more than a date or two and a few laughs. Why, she didn't know. She told herself it was because she wasn't as ruthless as Ramona and had mixed emotions about this whole stupid plan of hers.

But this was a fight for survival, she sternly reminded herself. And a man of the world like Sam could surely hold his own against a small-town vamp like Patty. Shaking off her feelings of guilt, Libby rolled up her sleeves, both literally and figuratively. She grabbed her clutch purse and headed out the door to the formidable task that lay ahead. First on her agenda, of course, was fetching Sam. Next, she had to nab a minute alone with George so she could find out where Patty hung out these days. Then she had to figure out a way to get her boss and second cousin together.

What a mess.

"Ramona, you're dead."

The ride down the mountain to Morrilton was as gorgeous as always. The brisk autumn breeze that teased the last colorful leaves from the trees also choreographed the cloud shadows waltzing across the soy bean and wheat fields on either side of Highway 154. Libby smiled her contentment as she drove the van eastward. Arkansas born and bred, she loved every square mile of the Natural State and intended to live to a ripe old age on the mountain she loved.

If Sam Knight didn't sell her home out from under her, that is. Her smile fading at that distressing thought, Libby sighed lustily. To occupy her troubled mind, she flipped on the radio, rewarded for her efforts by the haunting strains of a song that always brought a sentimental tear to her eye. Written for the Arkansas Sesquicentennial a few years back and adopted as one of the state songs, the lyrics of "Arkansas (You Run Deep in Me)" brought vividly to mind her happy childhood on Petit Jean. Intense determination flooded through her. Libby's last doubts about sic-ing Patty on Sam vanished. She had to do it. That was that.

When she reached Morrilton, the largest town in the immediate area, Libby made a quick stop at the printer's to pick up new menus for the restaurant. She turned into George's graveled parking lot barely ten minutes later, waving to her fifty-plus-year-old cousin as she stepped out of the van. Libby noted that Sam was nowhere to be seen and, taking advantage of that stroke of luck, hurried over to George to give him a hello hug.

"Hi there, stranger," she teased. "I haven't seen you or your gorgeous wife in ages. How've you two been?"

"Great. What about you?"

"Pretty great, myself. What's that daughter of yours up to these days?"

George grinned at Libby's unwitting choice of words, brushing back his bushy gray hair with a hand calloused from years of manual labor. "No good, I expect, but she comes by it honest."

"I'd sure love to see her," Libby said, hoping he would volunteer Patty's whereabouts. He didn't disappoint her.

"Then why don't you stop by the fairgrounds on your way out? She's working one of the charity booths today."

"I forgot all about the fair being in town," Libby said, adding, "I'll certainly have to go by there. Wouldn't want to miss my yearly candy apple." Not to mention this wonderful chance to introduce Sam to Patty, she added silently.

"I'm not sure your rider's in any mood for a carnival," George warned, glancing toward the brick building off to their right. "I just told him he's got over three thousand worth of damage to his Jaguar."

"Oh no," Libby moaned, scanning the area and immediately spotting the sleek black car, still hooked up to the wrecker. Her stomach knotted when she spotted the right front fender, now a mass of twisted metal, and then glanced toward the shop just in time to see Sam step out of the dark interior of the garage. He nodded when she waved, walking over to join them.

"Bad news, huh?" Libby prompted to break the sudden awkward silence.

"Worse than that," Sam replied.

"Well, at least you weren't hurt, and if it's any consolation, there's no better body man around than George."

"Thanks, Libby," George said with a self-conscious grin. "But I've already told your boss, here, that I don't have the parts he needs. Sam has decided to get the car repaired in Memphis."

"It's driveable?" Libby blurted, her head filled with visions of Sam disappearing into the sunset before she—or Patty—could change his mind.

"Will be by Monday afternoon," George promised.

Libby swallowed hard, amazed at the depth of the relief washing over her. She suddenly wondered if the uncertain fate of Wildwood was the sole reason for that attack of nerves, but lost that fleeting thought when Sam extended his hand to George and voiced his appreciation for the help. After promising to call as soon as the car was fit for travel,

George said his goodbyes and headed briskly for the shop, which should have closed a good hour before.

Libby and Sam walked to the van together without speaking. Sam, totally disgusted with himself for wrecking his car, got into the vehicle to sit in stony silence, arms crossed over his chest, while Libby situated herself behind the wheel. She flashed him a smile as she inserted the key into the ignition. He barely mustered the enthusiasm to smile back, managing nothing more than a poor imitation of the real thing.

She didn't seem to notice, however, putting the van into gear and pulling out onto the road. Libby talked nonstop as she drove—about the weather, which was perfect, about her family, which was large, and about some cousin named Patty.

Sam learned that Libby was the second of four children, with an older brother and two younger sisters, all of whom were married with children. Her father, who had wed quite young, was only forty-nine, her mother, forty-seven. Parents and siblings all lived within twenty miles, and, from the sound of things, were closely knit.

Sam, staring out the window, let her words wash over him, registering only half of what she said. His thoughts were on his car and the money he could have saved if the weather and the darkness hadn't conspired against him. He could only hope George knew what he was doing.

Lost in his thoughts, it took Sam several seconds to register that Libby had stopped talking. He experienced a moment's unease, wondering if she'd asked some question requiring an answer, and glanced her way. Her full attention seemed to be on her driving, however. Relieved, Sam used this oppertunity to inspect more closely the colorful outfit she wore. His eyes swept her willowy body, lingering where they had no business. Deliberately he raised his gaze, noting she'd braided her silky hair again. That brought vividly to mind their little collision last night. He tensed slightly, remembering how soft her skin had felt, how good she had smelled. His heart began to thud erratically.

At that moment Libby intercepted his intense stare. She glanced down at herself. "What's wrong?"

"Nothing," he blurted, chagrined at having been caught ogling her. "I was just, um... Nice outfit." Nice? Ha. Who was he kidding? She looked sexy as hell.

Dead silence greeted his stammering, unintentional compliment. Then Libby murmured, "Thanks." She coughed slightly, cleared her throat and said, "I need to make one quick stop before we head back—if you don't mind, that is."

"I don't mind," Sam replied, remembering she'd mentioned having some errands to run. He wondered briefly if Ramona had kept her promise not to tell Libby about his plans to sell the resort until everything was finalized, and he decided she must have. Libby would surely have challenged his decision by now if she knew.

Barely a quarter of a mile later, Libby turned off the highway into a crowded parking lot. Curious, Sam scanned the vaguely familiar area, immediately spotting the sign that read Conway County Fair. A few yards in the distance he saw the tents, booths and rides so typical of the fairs that traveled through the South in the autumn. Memories washed over him—memories of dust, cotton candy, music and ... girls. Lots of girls. He smiled to himself.

"George told me the fair was in town," Libby explained once she'd brought the van to a halt. "And I refuse to go back home without a candy apple. Want to walk with me?"

Sam did—just to see if things had changed since his teenage days.

Clearly pleased by his nod of agreement, Libby scrambled out of the van. Sam followed suit and in seconds found himself on the midway. As the two of them threaded their way through the milling throng of funseekers, Sam calculated how many years had passed since he'd set foot on that ground. He realized it had been a good twenty. Yet little had changed in that time.

Excited children still darted between dawdling adults, spilling popcorn, begging for more. Sly barkers still issued their colorful challenges. Hapless teenage boys still accepted them, squandering hard-earned cash on games of chance and skill in hopes of winning a stuffed animal to present to their young misses. How many times had he, himself, been in that position, Sam wondered, paying double what one of those teddy bears was worth in hopes of a thank-you kiss?

He grinned at the memory and glanced over at Libby. That grin vanished when he realized she watched him closely, taking note, no doubt, of his sappy sentimentality. Feigning an indifference he didn't feel, he hooked a thumb through a belt loop.

"Where are the apples?" he asked, somewhat gruffly, raising up to peer over the crowd.

"Way over there," Libby told him, threading her way through the crush. She greeted everyone she passed, taking time to introduce Sam to a good many of them. Finally, he spotted the concession, but before they could get to it, Libby whirled to face him, halting their progress.

"Oh, look!" she exclaimed, pointing off to their left. "The Tilt-A-Whirl. I haven't ridden that in years." She grabbed his hand, tugging him in that direction. "Want to ride it with me?"

"No thanks," he replied, digging his heels into the ground beneath their feet.

"Are you chicken?" Libby taunted him.

"No. I just don't enjoy that sort of thing."

"Come on," she wheedled. "I don't want to ride it by myself. Please, please, please?"

How could he resist those pleading brown eyes? "Just once," he heard himself say. "I'm too old for this sort of foolishness."

"Thanks, Gramps," Libby teased with an impish smile that did amazing things to his blood pressure.

Sam followed her to the ride, shaking his head in rueful disbelief. With serious second thoughts, he took his place in the short line, watching the cars that dipped and spun on a circular track set several feet off the ground. His stomach lurched at the sight, a fact that surprised him since he'd actually lied about not enjoying "that sort of thing." As a youngster, he'd considered no ride too challenging.

In no time, he found himself sitting beside Libby, thigh-to-thigh on the cracked vinyl seat. A scruffy-looking youth walked around each metal enclosure, inspecting the safety bar that lay across the laps of his victims. That accomplished, the attendant then took his place by the muffler-less motor, which putt-putted and then exploded into life, assaulting Sam's ears and sending the cars whirling and lurching around the track. Though under other circumstances, Sam would have relished the sensation of Libby struggling not to land in his lap, he didn't now. Instead, his stomach churned again, and he closed his eyes to blot out the blur of sky, ground and humanity swirling around him.

He thought the spinning ride would never end. When it finally did, he barely managed to crawl out of the car. Libby's excited laughter and flushed cheeks told him she had enjoyed every minute of the experience. Grasping the handrail, he descended the exit steps on legs downright wobbly. Baffled by this embarrassing reaction to what was, after all, a child's amusement, he halted a few feet from the Tilt-A-Whirl to regain his breath...and equilibrium. But the world continued to rotate, his head to swim.

"Are you all right?" Libby asked.

"Of course, I am," he replied. "Why?"

"Your face is the color of pea soup," she told him, her eyes beginning to twinkle mischievously. "Want to sit down for a minute?"

"No, I do not want to sit down for a minute," he snapped, certain she thought him a real wimp. "I want to buy that damned apple so we can get out of here."

"Okay, okay. Keep your hat on." Libby pivoted sharply in the direction of the candy-apple booth, marvelling at the size of the male ego. Obviously he was sick. Why didn't he just admit it, for Pete's sake?

"Libby?" Sam's voice sounded strained.

"What?" she demanded impatiently, turning to confront him.

"I think I'm going to throw up."

Chapter Three

Don't you dare!" Libby exclaimed. She hooked her arm through Sam's, hauling him to a bench at the edge of the midway. "Sit down. I'm getting you something cold to drink."

Sam didn't argue, Libby trotted over to a nearby refreshment stand, purchasing a cold soft drink that she thrust at him moments later. He put it to his lips immediately, tipping his head back to down the icy contents in one huge gulp. Within seconds, color flooded back into his face. Sam didn't move a muscle for a minute or two, then glanced up at Libby, who stood frowning down at him, hands on her hips. Intercepting her accusing stare, he sheepishly shrugged one shoulder.

"Why didn't you just tell me you have a weak stomach?" Libby demanded.

"Because I don't," Sam retorted, glaring back at her. He annihilated the paper cup in his hand and hurled it into the trash can.

"Right," she murmured dryly, rolling her eyes heaven-ward. Men. Who needed them or their macho pride? She studied Sam's stony expression, noting that his color had returned to normal . . . and then some. An angry flush now stained his cheeks. That, she abruptly decided, was reason enough to abandon her plans to introduce him to Patty. Romance was definitely out of the picture today. She could forsake Ramona's idiotic idea with a clear conscience.

And what about Wildwood? that same conscience de-manded of her. What about all those friends and relatives who would lose their jobs? Even if she was willing to toss her own future out the window, didn't she owe them at least one good try?

"Will you look at that!"

Sam's exclamation burst into Libby's abstraction of in-decision. She turned in the direction he pointed. "Look at what?"

"That Haunted House. I haven't been through one of those in years." His eyes were glued to the ghoulishly dec-orated structure.

"I've *never* been through one," Libby said, caught off guard by his sudden mood swing. She regretted her thoughtless admission when Sam's face lit up malevolently.

"Is that so?" He got to his feet, laying an arm heavily across her shoulders. "Come on. We've got a date with Count Dracula."

"But you're sick," Libby protested.

Sam ignored her comment, firmly urging her to the ticket booth. Reluctant to make a scene, Libby went along with him . . . until he actually paid admission for two and began to push her up the entrance ramp. The interior of the house, dark as a barrel of black cats and twice as spooky, loomed ahead. Libby's heart leapt into her throat.

"Look," she told him, catching hold of the hand rail to stop their progress. "I'm sorry if I bruised your ego a minute ago. You really don't have to prove anything to me."

"Don't be ridiculous, I merely want to see if they've changed these things since I was a kid."

"Then be my guest. I'll wait for you right over there."

"Are you chicken?" Sam asked, echoing her earlier taunt.

"Cluck-cluck," she replied with a brisk nod. "And *not* into being frightened out of my wits."

"Turnabout is fair play," he reminded her. "I rode that stupid ride with you. The least you can do is return the courtesy and walk through this with me."

Libby hesitated. Obviously sensing her inner struggle, Sam pointed to a child of about six or seven years, just exiting the building, all smiles. "How scary can it be?"

That was exactly what Libby wanted to know. When several other young children burst out the door, laughing wildly and with all their limbs intact, she reluctantly acknowledged that she just might have watched too many horror movies as a foolhardy teenager. Abruptly she gave in, slightly embarrassed at having made such a fuss. "You're right. How scary *can* it be?"

She found out a heart thump later when Sam disappeared into the pitch-black interior. Sucking in a fortifying breath, Libby followed. The wooden floor beneath their feet creaked loudly with every step, dipping when she least expected it, hindering her progress down what seemed to be a hallway. She couldn't tell for sure and had to feel her way along. Afraid she might get separated from Sam, whose steady footfall mocked her stumbling one, Libby reached out, groping for him in the dark. Her fingertips first connected with the nicely-rounded back pockets of his jeans. Muttering an apology, she located his leather belt a little higher up and then a belt loop, through which she hooked her forefinger.

He didn't verbally acknowledge that display of cowardice, but when they found their way into an area eerily lighted by a solitary red bulb, she saw he had a grin on his face. Libby refused to let him get to her, however, and shamelessly tightened her hold. With some reluctance she scanned the tiny room into which they'd stepped, gasping when her gaze met that of a pasty-faced vampire, lurking in a deep shadow just over her shoulder. He smiled a black-lipped smile and took one menacing step her way before Libby screeched and bounded for the nearest door. She threw it open wide, leaping through, an action that nearly tripped Sam, whose belt-loop she still clutched in a death-grip.

The door shut behind with a bone-chilling squeal. Once again intense dark enveloped them, softened only by a ghostly blue glow beckoning from up ahead. Libby heard Sam's soft chuckle.

"This isn't funny!" she snapped, one hand on her heart to make sure it hadn't jumped right out of her chest.

He made no response, moving relentlessly on. Groans and screams emanated from the walls on either side of them. A giant spider dangled before her eyes.

Ducking, Libby abandoned the belt loop and slipped her hand into Sam's. Though he didn't speak, he laced his fingers with hers. The blue grew brighter with every step forward. Together they stepped into another chamber, this one a crypt decorated with Egyptian hieroglyphics. An open sarcophagus stood in one corner. Libby closed her eyes, certain the tattered mummy inside it was going to spring to life and attack. But it didn't. When several uneventful seconds passed, she gingerly opened one eye... just as something grabbed her from behind.

Shrieking her terror, Libby never looked back, fleeing the room in record time, dragging Sam with her into the next hallway. He laughed openly now. "Isn't this great?"

"Oh, hush up," she muttered, wrapping both arms around his waist and burying her face in his shoulder. Still laughing, Sam moved them steadily toward a closed door, which exuded a flashing white light. The hallway narrowed alarmingly. Sam turned slightly so they could maneuver through it single file, an action that put Libby in the lead. Ruthlessly he propelled her to that door, which swung open as they approached.

Thoroughly spooked, Libby barely mustered the courage to risk a peek. When she did, she found herself inches from a hooded specter brandishing a chainsaw that erupted into earshattering violence. Libby screamed in horror, abandoning Sam to spring out the door to safety.

She found herself in yet another corridor, this one bathed in sunlight. The exit lay a couple of yards ahead. Not quite ready to face the world, Libby leaned against the wall, giving her jellied knees a much needed break. A second later, Sam joined her.

"How're you doin'?" he asked, visibly struggling with a smile.

"Just dandy," she told him, irritated by his amusement. She could see he thought this whole experience hilarious, and she felt an utter fool for having acted like such a baby.

"You should have told me you don't like this sort of thing."

"I did tell you, dammit."

Chuckling, Sam suddenly tugged Libby to him, wrapping his arms tightly around her. Startled by the unexpected, lung-crushing hug, she tried to squirm free. But he wouldn't let her.

Libby wedged her hands between them, desperately struggling to draw in enough breath to tell him off. She raised her chin. Their gazes met and melded. In slow motion Sam lowered his head, touching his mouth to hers in a feather-soft kiss that tasted of lemon-lime and laughter. Shocked to the bone, Libby tensed in his arms, only one coherent thought surfacing through the waves of sensation that swirled around and over her...*don't stop.*

But he did, releasing her a millisecond later and stepping abruptly back. His gasps for air mingled with hers. Their eyes met again, a heart-stopping collision of topaz and sapphire. With a groan, he reached out for her. She met him halfway, throwing her arms around his neck, raising on her tiptoes to press her body and mouth to his.

His probing tongue parted her eager lips. Libby opened her mouth to his hungry kiss, letting him devour at will. Then, when he was satiated, she became the epicure, sampling the flavor that was so distinctly Sam.

But this time the kiss tasted of danger. Suddenly unsure of herself, Libby sagged against him. He willingly supported her and trailed his lips over her cheek, seeking the ultrasensitive flesh just below her ear. When she shivered in response, he raised his head and frowned at her.

"You're not still scared, are you?"

"Scared?" Libby echoed absently, vampires, mummies and chainsaws now the last thing on her mind.

Sam grinned. "Let's go get that apple." He took her hand, holding on until they stepped out onto the exit, when he released her. Side-by-side, they walked toward the concession stand. Lost in her tumultuous thoughts, Libby spoke to no one, this time never even registering the greetings of the friends and acquaintances passing on either side.

I can't believe he did that, she mused. *I can't believe I did that.* So what now? Obviously he wasn't the monk his sister thought him to be. If she took him to Patty, would the two of them hit it off? More important, did Libby even want them to?

She realized with a shock that she wasn't so sure. She thought of the fiery kiss they'd just shared and wondered if maybe she shouldn't take Ramona's original advice and do the dirty work herself. If the last few minutes were anything to go by, it might not take much effort at all to remind Sam how magical romance could be.

Romance? Libby winced, knowing full well romance had nothing whatsoever to do with what had just transpired between the two of them. That was pure sexual attraction—unexpected, unexplainable, unwanted. And since she obviously had no sense at all where this man was concerned, Libby knew she would be playing with fire if she tried to take on the likes of Sam Knight. That left only Patty.

When Libby and Sam reached the concession stand, she bought two of the cellophane-wrapped apples, bright red and utterly luscious looking. Very casually, Libby asked directions to the dunking booth, which turned out to be about halfway back to the parking lot on the other side of the looped midway.

"Mind if we go back a different way?" Libby asked, pocketing her change. "I'd like to say hello to a cousin of mine, George's daughter, Patty Milam. I promised him I would."

Sam patiently shrugged his agreement. Libby led the way to the booth, stopping a few feet away from it to assess the situation. Redheaded, violet-eyed Patty looked as stunning as always seated on a wooden plank above a clear-sided water tank. Her one-piece bathing suit, which hugged every generous curve, exactly matched her wide eyes and set off to perfection a golden tan few other redheads could flaunt.

Patty called out to the passing crowd, attempting to lure prospective customers to the booth, sponsored by a local civic organization to benefit needy families in the area.

"Come on, honey," she called out to one particularly muscular male specimen. "I get off in ten minutes and it's Clyde the Clown up next. This is your last chance to dunk me."

Not surprisingly the man took her bait, stepping toward the booth. He handed the attendant a dollar bill, which entitled him to hurl two baseballs at a small bull's-eye several feet away. When the young man assumed a pitcher's stance, Patty squealed in mock terror, a sound that effectively destroyed his concentration and caused him to miss his target. Grumbling good naturedly, he tried again, but with no better luck. He then ambled off, laughingly refusing her challenge to invest another dollar.

Encouraged by this evidence of the effect a violet mermaid could have on the male species, Libby grabbed Sam's arm, leading him to the momentarily-deserted booth. She waved to Patty, who waved back. "Well, look who's here. How in the world are you?"

"Doing fine," Libby said. "How about you?"

"Not so bad now that the breeze has died down some. The water's cold, you know, and when I climb back out, I turn into one big goosebump." She smiled smugly and pushed back a lock of the russet hair curling damply around her face. "Luckily most of the guys I've attracted today couldn't hit the broad side of a barn with a base fiddle."

I wonder why, Libby thought, smiling back with difficulty since she'd now begun to have serious second thoughts about this whole idea. For some reason she couldn't bear the thought of Sam joining the ranks of the other jokers who'd lost their hearts, not to mention a buck, to her cousin that day. "Patty, I'd like you to meet Sam Knight, the owner of Wildwood. He's staying on Petit Jean this weekend."

"So *you're* the mastermind behind that wonderful resort," Patty crooned, her glowing eyes sweeping Sam once and then again.

"Actually Libby gets full credit," Sam tactfully murmured.

Patty laughed, obviously convinced he was just being modest. "Got a dollar, Sam? It's for a good cause."

When Sam shook his head, Libby gave him a playful push. "Aw, come on," she urged, to gauge his response to Patty. She knew from Ramona that he'd played baseball for years and figured that if he missed his target, she could consider herself on the right track. "I've seen those trophies of yours."

He hesitated and then dug into his pocket to extract a dollar, which he handed to a nearby attendant. Patty raised her chin and squared her shoulders, issuing a challenge no red-blooded male could ignore. That calculated move stretched the spandex suit even more tautly over her breasts. Her full lips widened into a sultry smile that proclaimed victory before the battle even began. Libby's stomach churned. She closed her eyes, suddenly unwilling to witness Sam's demise.

A thud and a splash later, her eyes flew open again to see that Sam had hit the target and, Patty, the water. Laughing good-naturedly, the redhead scrambled from the tank via a ladder and resumed her position once again, playfully threatening Sam with a raised fist.

He'll never be able to do it again, Libby thought, eyeing the shimmery bathing suit which now clung wetly. Patty tossed back her hair, assumed a pose worthy of a *Sports Illustrated* swimsuit layout and called out, "Go for it."

A second later she hit the water again, sending skyward a spray of droplets. Instead of resuming her perch, Patty scooped up a towel when she climbed out of the tank and walked over to join Sam and Libby. Libby guessed her cousin found Sam's apparent immunity to her charms quite intriguing.

"Good shot!" Patty gushed with a smile that said all was forgiven. Making a great show of drying her lithe body, she then announced that she was off duty and could be dressed in no time, if they wanted to stick around for a while.

"Can't do it," Sam said before Libby had a chance to respond.

"We can't?" she blurted, not quite believing her ears or what she had just witnessed.

"We can't."

"Oh." Libby, noting the determined set of his jaw, turned to Patty then, shrugging an apology. "Sorry. We really have to hit the road. I just stopped by to get these—" she held up the apples "—and say hello."

Clearly disappointed, Patty nodded. "Maybe another time?"

"Maybe," Sam said, taking Libby's arm and leading her none-too-gently away. He kept silent until they got to the van, where he held out his hand, palm upward. "Keys."

Libby didn't argue, tossing them to him. He unlocked the passenger side and opened the door. "You eat. I'll drive."

She climbed up into the van and reached over to unlock his door. He got in behind the steering wheel, inserted the key and put the vehicle in motion. Five minutes later found them on the highway once more, headed to Wildwood.

"Now then," Sam said, flicking an accusing glance her way. "Would you like to tell me what that was all about?" Instead of answering him, Libby ripped the cellophane from one of the apples. She took a big bite out of it, rewarded for her efforts by a gooey red mustache and a mouthful of ambrosia, which made it conveniently impossible to talk. With a snarl of impatience, Sam fished into his pocket for a handkerchief, tossing it in her direction.

Twenty-five minutes later—Sam was counting rather impatiently—when Libby finally swallowed the last sticky bite and could talk again, he turned the van off the highway onto one of the many lookouts along the scenic drive up the mountain. Sam killed the engine and swiveled to face Libby, noting her mahogany eyes were huge with dread.

"Okay. Talk."

"Excuse me?"

"I want to know what you're up to."

"I'm not *up to* anything," she told him, but she couldn't meet his gaze.

"Like hell you're not. Now I want the truth. What's the deal with Patty? Why did you drag me over to that dunking booth, and don't tell me it was to say hello to her. Even an idiot could see you two don't get along, and contrary to what my sister's honeymoon hoax may have led you to think, I'm not one of those."

Her cheeks as red as the apple she'd just consumed, Libby shrugged defeat. "All right then, I'll tell you. This morning Ramona spilled your plans to sell Wildwood. She believes your decision has something to do with the fact that you've forgotten how wonderful romance can be—probably because you haven't dated in so long. Anyway, she . . . *we* decided to try to hook you up with someone who could remind you."

"Patty?" he questioned through gritted teeth.

Libby nodded.

"Of all the harebrained—" Sam drew in a steadying breath and sat on his hands to keep from shaking some sense into Ramona by proxy. "Contrary to what my dear sister thinks, I do date. Not as often as I once did, but *I do date*."

"You do?"

"You're damned right I do, and I haven't forgotten how won—" he just couldn't say it—" *entertaining* romance can be."

"You haven't?"

"Hell, no. I just don't have time for that kind of foolishness these days." He reached out to start the engine again, leaving the lookout with a spray of gravel. A mile farther down the road, he flicked a glance in her direction, noting she was looking out the window, nervously gnawing her full bottom lip. That brought to mind the kisses they'd shared not so very long ago. The intense desire he'd felt for her washed over him again, and it was all he could do not to stop the van and take her into his arms to see if another kiss would appease the aching need inside him.

But she was looking for moonlight and roses, he sternly reminded himself, knowing he yearned for something different. Oh, it wasn't as though he'd always been such a cynic about romance. He hadn't. In fact he couldn't even count all the times he'd surprised his wife with flowers during their three-year marriage, not to mention the bottles of wine, the sinfully sexy lingerie . . .

But it was never enough, a fact she demonstrated quite clearly when she dumped him for another man—a man willing to sacrifice his soul, which was the only thing Sam had refused to give her. Sam vowed then that he would never again make a fool of himself like that. He hadn't, either, dating only when he couldn't stand the solitude of his empty house a second longer, and then never the same woman more than once.

He had his head on straight these days and had for years. Divorce court had merely strengthened his resolve to go it alone—free, wholehearted and, if the truth be admitted, damned frustrated. And that frustration, Sam decided, was undoubtedly the reason he'd kissed Libby. He was a normal male, after all. It wasn't so surprising that being close to her there in the dark had proved his undoing.

And what a kiss. He'd felt it clear to his toenails, a fact that rankled since the kiss had obviously meant little to Libby. Hadn't she tried to pawn him off on Patty *after* it? Did that mean he was the only one attracted here? Or had he merely grown rusty in the art of lovemaking—a problem a little more practice might solve? Suddenly he had to know.

"Libby?"

"Hmm?"

"Why did you drag Patty into this? Why didn't *you* take me on? I am stuck up here all weekend, and you must know I—" He broke off abruptly, thinking better of what he'd almost admitted.

"Ramona wanted me to," Libby said, apparently unaware of his near slipup. "But I told her no."

"Oh, you did, huh?"

"I did. I'm not your type, you're not mine. I couldn't see wasting the weekend."

"You call fighting for Wildwood wasting the weekend?"

"No, I call *me* trying to romance *you* wasting the weekend."

"Why?" Sam demanded, swerving to avoid a rock that had rolled down the side of the mountain.

"Do you really want to know?"

"Yes."

"Swear you won't laugh?"

"Yes."

"I have, a time or two, been called a romantic—"

"Nawww!" he teased, immediately regretting it when she glared at him.

"*And* I've been nagged about waiting so long to get married."

"Always the bridesmaid, never the bride?"

"Please, not you, too," she groaned. "I'm single by choice. I have been asked—and more than once."

"So what are you waiting for?" he prompted, oddly curious.

"A man who believes in the things I believe in. A man who holds love and marriage in the same high regard as I do."

Sam snorted his impatience with the unreality of her expectations. "And what's that got to do with me?" he asked as he turned off the highway onto a narrower side road.

"I decided long ago not to waste my time on any man I wouldn't marry. That way I can be sure I won't fall for the wrong guy."

He grinned at the very idea of proposing to her—marriage, anyway. "And that's why you didn't take me on—because you wouldn't marry me?"

"No," she said. "I didn't take you on because I was afraid I might fall for you."

Libby's candid admission hit Sam like a ton of bricks. Stunned, he swiveled his gaze in her direction, rewarded for his distraction by the crunch of gravel as the right front tire dropped smack off the road. Muttering a curse, Sam yanked the steering wheel back to the left with difficulty.

"No wonder you had a wreck last night," Libby commented, grabbing the dash in a white-knuckled clench to keep from falling off the seat.

Still recovering from the bombshell she'd just dropped, Sam didn't even hear her. She might fall for him? Hot damn. That meant he hadn't lost his touch. That meant she just might be as attracted as he was.

And that meant . . . trouble. He swallowed hard.

"I just can't believe you'd sell this place," Libby commented, gesturing to a large billboard that exactly matched the one Sam had seen in Little Rock the day before.

"Believe it," he told her.

"Why did you even buy Wildwood?"

"I didn't buy Wildwood," he replied. He shifted slightly to better see both her and the road. "I bought Cedar Ridge Resort."

She winced. "All right, then, why did you buy Cedar Ridge?"

"As an investment. I thought that with a little work it might make me some money."

"And hasn't it?" Libby asked, turning to lean back on the door and tucking one leg underneath her.

"So far."

"Then what's the problem?" She'd crossed her arms over her chest and looked prepared to stay that way forever, if that's what it took to get an answer.

Sam didn't intend to take that long. "The problem is all the corny romance-can-save-your-marriage hype naturally associated with a place like this. We both know that once a married couple steps out of the sanctuary of Wildwood, reality will hit twice as hard. People naturally change through the years, and it's unrealistic to believe that any man and woman will fall in love and stay that way for the rest of their lives."

"That's not true!" Libby said emotionally. "Why, if you keep romance in a relationship—make an honest effort to hold on to the magic of that first-time feeling—you can't help but succeed." She leaned forward and shook her finger at Sam. "There are millions of happy marriages out there. You've lost your perspective—steeped yourself in the failures. Why, I—"

"All right, all right, I get your drift," Sam interjected, holding up a hand to halt the heated rush of words. He made a quick inspection of Libby's face, missing not one detail of her flushed cheeks and flashing brown eyes. Her full lips, pursed in a near pout, begged to be kissed again, *God, but she's gorgeous,* he thought just as he shocked them both by muttering, "I won't sell out . . . *if* you'll change the focus. I cannot, in good conscience, make money off both honeymoons *and* divorces. It's intolerable. Hell, it's worse than intolerable. It's unethical."

"But if you change the focus, you'll have just another run-of-the-mill motel," Libby argued, throwing her hands up in impatience. "Wildwood is the perfect place to begin a marriage and the perfect place to escape the problems that can rip one apart. Our guests come here deliberately, by mutual consent, knowing they'll find peace, quiet and, if they try real hard, each other."

"That's garbage!" Sam exclaimed, slapping the steering wheel to make his point.

Libby snorted her exasperation. "Ramona sure had you pegged right."

"What do you mean?" Sam demanded, bristling. "What'd she say?"

"She called you a Scrooge," Libby retorted. "And after hearing that bah-humbug theory of yours, I think she's right."

"Well, Scrooge or not, my mind is made up."

Libby drew in a deep breath and then let it slowly back out. "Isn't there anything I can say to convince you how wonderful romance can be?"

Your place or mine might do the trick, Sam thought, relishing the sight of her heaving chest. At once, he bemoaned that unspoken reply. Two little kisses. That's all it had taken to turn a levelheaded divorce attorney into a weak-kneed wimp. Maybe Ramona was smarter than he thought. Maybe he *had* gone it alone too long.

"Nothing," Sam told Libby, with new determination. He refused to let his loneliness get the better of his good sense.

She tilted her head, clearly deep in thought. "You know," she said after a moment's silence. "I'd have expected better from a man like you."

"What the hell is that supposed to mean?"

"You're a lawyer, for Pete's sake. Yet you've reached your verdict without even taking a look at all the evidence."

Sam realized with a pang of guilt that she spoke the truth.

"I deserve an opportunity to present my case," Libby persisted as though sensing his dilemma. "Let me have the rest of your weekend to show you around Wildwood. You're going to be there anyway."

That he was, and his strong sense of fairness dictated that she be given the chance to plead her cause. "Can I expect to be visited by the ghosts of marriage past, present and future if I do?"

Refusing to let him bait her, Libby didn't answer.

Sam's shoulders sagged in defeat. "Oh, all right, I'll hold off on a final decision until Monday, but don't get your hopes up. I'm a hard man, and I can be damned ruthless when I think I'm right. I'm not going to be easy to convince."

That said, Sam braked sharply, jerking the steering wheel to the right to take to the shoulder of the road again. Before Libby could demand an explanation, he put the van in park, stepped out and strode to a spot in the middle of the road just ahead. To Libby's amazement, he scooped up a large map turtle she hadn't even seen and walked to the edge of the pavement, where he deposited it in the grass out of harm's way.

Some "hard man," Libby thought, grinning her delight. Her spirits lifted. Victory was surely hers.

Chapter Four

Look at this. Just look at this," Sam muttered as he drove the van into the parking lot of Wildwood a few minutes afterward. "There are two, four, six...*ten* cars here with Just Married smeared all over them. God, that's disgusting. Don't those poor idiots know the divorce rate? Why, within a year, four of those ten couples will be in some lawyer's office, ready—no, eager—to call it quits."

Her spirits taking a sudden nosedive, Libby bit back her rejoinder. There was no sense in bandying words with a man who made his living arguing...especially one this cynical. She would do better to direct her energies toward something more constructive, namely plotting her campaign. Libby had won a major victory by getting Sam to give her his weekend. She intended to make use of every minute.

"I've got to take some menus to the restaurant," Libby said, changing the subject very deliberately. "Then I'm going to clean up your cabin. Why don't you take a stroll by the lake until I get finished?"

"You don't have a maid who could do that for you?"

"Yes, I do—my Aunt Cecilia. Unfortunately she got off at four, and since I forgot to ask my cousin to tell her about unit six needing a clean up, it probably wasn't touched." Libby climbed out of the van, pausing a moment to hug Fetch, who'd bounded up to greet her, before she walked to the back of the vehicle.

"Sounds like Wildwood is a family affair," Sam commented, joining Libby. When he spotted Fetch, he grinned and dropped to his knee to give the big black canine a scratch behind the ears.

"It is," Libby told him, opening the doors and reaching in for the box of menus. "I have eight relatives working here with me."

"No wonder you're so anxious to maintain the norm," Sam murmured, ducking the dog's pink tongue. He stood to take the box from her.

"That and the fact that I love it here. I don't know what I'll do if you sell out and I have to leave." Libby started across the parking lot to the restaurant.

"Why would you have to leave?" Sam called after her. "You're obviously capable. I'll give you a good recommendation."

"Many motel chains have their own training programs these days," Libby replied over her shoulder. "And that includes both of the companies who have made offers on Wildwood."

"I didn't know that," Sam murmured as he stepped past Libby to enter the restaurant.

"Just put them there," Libby said, pointing to a table near the swinging kitchen doors. Sam did as she asked, and in seconds they were back outside, Libby once more in the lead. "Thanks. Now you run along and play. I have work to do."

"I'm going to help," Sam said.

"No, you aren't. That's my job. You're the guest."

"I'm the *owner*," he corrected coldly. "For now, anyway. And what I say goes."

With a sharp salute, Libby acknowledged his authority. She and Sam headed to unit six, via a storage closet full of brooms, mops and cleaning supplies. Arms laden, the two of them then walked to the cabin where Sam had slept the night before.

Libby took a quick look around and set to work immediately, with Sam's help, clearing the room of all the trash and dust that had accumulated since the cabin had been under repair. They next concentrated their efforts on rearranging that area, pushing excess furniture into the bedroom and dragging out of it the king-sized mattresses and headboard, which had been propped against the wall to make room for the workmen. That accomplished, they reassembled the bed and made it up.

Fetch supervised their every move, of course, more than once poking his cold, curious nose where it didn't belong. In spite of him, however, the end result was a fairly neat livingroom-bedroom combination. Sam, clearly pleased with the result, verbalized his approval, immediately spoiling that treasured compliment with a grumbled complaint about the state of the bathroom.

Holding her ready temper in check, Libby made short work of that little chore. In minutes the white-and-yellow tile walls and floor, not to mention the hot tub and shower, had been rid of a layer of sawdust and shone like new money. On a roll, she next tackled the kitchen, and that in spite of Sam's assurances he wouldn't be caught dead in there.

"You don't cook?" Libby asked as she sprayed the counters with an all-purpose cleanser and wiped it down.

"I took my turn in the kitchen until my divorce," he said, adding, "Then I hired a live-in housekeeper."

"I know it's none of my business," Libby ventured, "But did you leave your wife or vice versa?"

"You're right, it's none of your business," Sam told her.

Momentarily tabling her quest to find out if his own divorce had contributed to his negative attitude, Libby finished up her chores without further small talk. Finally, she pirouetted to inspect the room, dusted her hands together and announced, "All done." She glanced at her watch. "And it's only five. There's still plenty of time to give you the grand tour before dark."

"Aw, Libby. I really don't—"

"None of that," she interjected, cutting off Sam's attempted refusal. "You gave me your weekend."

"Okay, okay," he muttered with a face that said quite clearly he already regretted that rash gift.

"We'll start with the swimming pool," Libby said. "It's heated now, you know." She led Sam and her beloved dog toward the door and down the porch steps in the direction of a tall privacy fence.

The sun, just beginning to sink behind gold-rimmed cumulus clouds, glowed red-orange in the sky. Sam breathed deeply of the air, so crisp and clear, smiling to himself with pleasure. He loved Petit Jean Mountain. Always had. He especially loved the state park, just three miles farther down the highway. As a troubled teenager floundering in the backwash of his parent's bitter divorce and as an adult experiencing the trauma of his own, Sam had escaped to it often, camping for days, hiking the trails, exploring the caves. He'd found peace there, peace just like he felt right now. It was like coming home.

He had to give Libby credit, he reluctantly acknowledged as his gaze swept the unobtrusive log cabins on all sides. The resort detracted not one whit from the natural charm of the densely wooded area. She had done a fine job renovating. Too bad she'd gummed up the works with all that love-can-last-forever malarkey.

Libby pulled open the gate of the wooden fence, ordering her pet to stay and inviting Sam inside with a poolward sweep of her arm. He stepped through the gate, where he paused for a moment, orienting to the new surroundings. He saw that the pool area was deserted except for a man and a woman, seated at one of several wrought-iron patio tables to one side of the sparkling blue water. They waved to Libby, who took Sam's arm, leading him over to them. To his embarrassment she then proceeded to introduce him as the owner of the resort.

"I'm so pleased to meet you, Mr. Knight," the woman, a petite brunette who looked to be in her mid-forties, gushed. "I want to congratulate you on Wildwood. It's lovely. Just lovely. Arkansas has needed a resort like this for years."

"Yes, well thanks," Sam hedged, taken aback by her praise and highly conscious of Libby's smug smile.

"And you picked the perfect location," her gray-haired husband added. "So romantic, especially in light of Petit Jean's story. I'm sure you know it."

"I know it," Sam quickly replied, not the least bit interested in hearing yet again the legend of the Frenchwoman for whom the mountain was named. He'd never really seen anything romantic about a woman dressing as a man to follow her fiancé to the New World on a French exploration of the Louisiana Territory. Foolish would be a better word, he thought, or maybe tragic, since she had died on the mountain.

"We watched the sunrise from the grave site," the man said then. "It was breathtaking. We plan to come back here for our anniversary every year. In fact, I've already made reservations for next fall."

"Is that so?" Sam murmured, embarrassed by such a blatant display of sentimentality from a member of his own sex. "I'm, uh, glad to hear that. Thank you very much." Taking Libby's arm, he nodded a goodbye and practically dragged her inside the nearby building.

"Wasn't that sweet?" Libby asked, once they were out of earshot of their guests.

"Downright sticky," Sam wryly agreed.

Huffing her impatience with him, Libby took the lead down a short hallway to a room labeled Sauna. Just as she reached for the doorknob, it turned. A young couple stepped out, voicing a greeting. As before, Libby introduced Sam as the owner of Wildwood. And as before, the enthusiastic compliments of the guests took him by surprise. Libby positively beamed by the time the two of them stuck their heads into the steamy sauna room to inspect it, and Sam couldn't really blame her. Clearly Wildwood was a hit. Clearly she thought she'd won her case.

But she hadn't and . . . wouldn't.

"Before you get your hopes up, I want to warn you that I'm not impressed by your guests' comments," Sam said, pulling off his glasses to defog them.

Her face fell. "You're not?"

"No. They're all a little crazy as far as I'm concerned. Haven't they just gotten *married*?"

"Oh, Sam," Libby murmured, slowly shaking her head. "You *are* a hard man." Reaching out a hand to stop him from replacing his glasses, she dug into her pants pocket to extract the handkerchief he'd loaned her earlier. Carefully folding it clean side out, Libby blotted the beads of perspiration that had broken out on his forehead.

Hit in the gut by her feather touch, Sam caught both her hands in his, imprisoning them against his suddenly pounding heart. That action kept her full lips temptingly close, further threatening his composure.

"I did try to warn you," he murmured huskily, wondering what she would do if he stole another kiss.

"So you did," she said, raising her dark-eyed gaze to meet his.

Sam's resistance wavered alarmingly. He swayed forward slightly and then regained control of himself, abruptly releasing her. "It would save us both a lot of trouble if you just went ahead and admitted defeat. I could round up a television or a good book, retreat to my cabin and stay there until Monday."

"Do you really want to do that?" Libby asked softly.

Sam found he couldn't lie. "No." Hastily he added, "I'm, uh, kind of enjoying this. I can hardly wait to find out what's next on the agenda."

Libby laughed with delight. "Actually there is no agenda. I'm making this up as I go along, and I could do a lot better job of it if you would give me a hint as to why you're so dead set against honeymoons. It has to be more than your line of work. I know policemen who don't consider everyone crooks and doctors who don't think we're all contagious. Surely you must know there are some happy marriages in this world."

"A few, maybe," Sam grumbled reluctantly.

"More than a few, and you know it. So come clean. Why are you so uptight about this? Is it because of your own divorce?"

"Mine . . . and that of my parents," he finally admitted, immediately wondering why he'd opened up to her. As a rule, he kept his personal affairs just that—strictly personal.

"Want to talk about it?" Libby asked.

"Not really," he said, "but since you're obviously not going to give me a moment's peace until I do..." He took her hand, leading her the few steps to a lounge area with an ice maker and vending machines. There he sat on the couch, tugging Libby down on the cushion next to him. "As you probably know, my parents divorced. Happened when I was in the tenth grade. They'd been fighting for years—as long as I can remember, now that I think about it. I was actually glad when Dad finally left."

"I'm so sorry," Libby murmured, closing the distance between them to slip her arm around his neck in a brief hug.

Sam shrugged and swallowed back the unwanted lump of emotion her sympathy had evoked. He hadn't talked about his parents' painful break-up in a very long time, and then only to Ramona, who'd been six when it happened and had never really understood how he felt about it.

"It was a long time ago," he murmured self-consciously. "I'm over it now."

"Are you? And what about *your* divorce? Tell me about that."

"What can I say? I met Claire, we got married, she split."

"I think you left something out," Libby said, crossing her legs and lacing her fingers together around her knee.

Sam frowned. "What's that?"

"Falling in love."

He laughed bitterly. "There's no such thing."

"Then why did you two get married in the first place?"

"The same reason most people get married, sex. I was young and hot-blooded, she was young and gorgeous."

"Hormones got the best of you, huh?"

Sam nodded. "Exactly."

"Well, it's no wonder you two didn't make it then. *Love*, not sex, is the key, Sam—the extra bit of ribbon that holds two people together when all other ties have been stressed to breaking point."

"And romance keeps love alive, right?" Sam asked, though he knew what her answer would be.

"Exactly!" Libby exclaimed, slapping the couch cushion. "I knew you'd catch on if I said it often enough."

"Actually, you've said it several times too many," Sam told her, getting to his feet. "And just for the record—I haven't caught on. Monogamy is an unnatural state. It is utterly crazy to expect two people to be happy together their whole lives. Now are we finished? I'd like to take a shower and—"

"Dress for dinner?" Libby interjected.

Sam groaned. "Dinner?"

"Uh-huh. Around seven, after our walk by the lake, which is after I show you through one of the cabins we're holding for late arrivals—newlyweds from Wichita, Kansas."

"I thought you didn't have an agenda," Sam accused.

"Actually...it's coming right along," Libby countered with a bubbly laugh.

Knowing there was no use in arguing, Sam merely nodded and followed her outside to a cabin nestled among some tall pines. He half listened to her rambling narrative about the renovation of this and that other cabin, his thoughts on their recent conversation. He felt as though he'd known Libby all his life, could tell her anything. It was almost as if she were a long-lost sister or something. Sister? Thank God, she wasn't, because his lustful thoughts that afternoon had been far from brotherly.

Minutes later, Libby stepped onto the wooden porch. Unable to help himself, Sam hung back a couple of steps to scope her outfit one more time. Then, fighting to get control of his misbehaving eyes and thoughts, he joined her. In seconds, they were inside the semidarkened cabin. Libby flipped on the overhead light, chasing the shadows of dusk to the corners of the room.

Biting back the exclamation of surprised approval that almost tumbled off his tougue, Sam somehow kept his face expressionless while he checked out the rustic livingroom. There were no polyester bearskins, just carpeting that captured the muted earthtones of the couch, wallpaper and curtains. A ruffled throw pillow and a ginger-jar lamp, both the exact shade of the waning sun outside, added a splash of color. The stone fireplace, filled with split logs ready to burn, and the low coffee table, spread with complimentary fruit, cheese and wine, lured him to relax and enjoy.

But it wasn't food or wine he craved. It was the taste of Libby's lips, full, slightly parted and sweeter than any wine. Her eyes sparkled with pride and anticipation of his approval. Sam couldn't deny her.

"Very nice," he murmured, refusing to commit himself further until he saw the bedroom. He still feared he might discover that heartshaped waterbed.

But he didn't. That room was decorated just as tastefully, this time in shades of ivory and country blue. It was, perhaps, a little too frilly for his taste with the eyelet Priscilla curtains and coverlet, but that was to be expected. A woman—a very feminine woman—had chosen the decor.

Sam eyed the big brass bed, his libido now running rampant. The covers had been pulled back, revealing softly patterned sheets and pillows. His heart constricted with longing he could neither explain or deny. How wonderful it would be to hide here with Libby, he thought, kissing, exploring.

He looked her way, wondering why he was so drawn to her. Was it something so simple as her beauty? Or was it more complex, like her obvious enthusiasm for her work?

Her optimism? The die-hard romantic in her? All of the above, he decided, next wondering what it would be like to come home every night to someone with such a positive outlook on life. He couldn't even imagine it. Claire had never been satisfied and made certain he wasn't, either. He hadn't lied when he said that the two of them hadn't loved each other.

Love? There was no such thing, just the physical attraction natural between the sexes. And therein lay the danger of Wildwood, he silently reiterated. It was just as he'd told Libby earlier; a honeymoon hideaway could easily lull a couple into a false sense of well-being. As a result, such facts of life as bills, sickness and parenting would be that much harder to handle once back in the stream of life.

Somehow he had to make Libby see the danger of this romantic resort. But how? Their hours together that day had revealed her stubbornness. Mere words would never convince her. *So I'll find another way,* he abruptly decided.

"Sam? Aren't you going to take a look in here?"

He dragged himself back to the present with difficulty, sticking his head into the huge bathroom. He noted it was much like the one in his unit, with a spacious closet, twin marble sinks, a shower and a hot tub.

Perfect, he thought, aloud murmuring nothing more than another brisk, "Very nice."

Visibly disappointed by his noncommital comment, Libby nonetheless managed a smile. "Thanks." She walked to the door and opened it. "Next up—the lake."

The lake, huh? he thought, following her outside. His eyes narrowed. He frowned thoughtfully, suddenly alert to the barest glimmerings of an idea as to how he just might teach Libby the cold, hard facts of life.

It was dusky dark by the time they reached the lake. The evening sky now ranged in color from deep mauve streaked with gold in the west to charcoal gray lightly sprinkled with stars in the east. Libby could almost smell a weather change in the air and hoped the cold front approaching from the northwest wouldn't bring with it more dreaded thunderstorms or even one of the tornadoes so common during Arkansas springs and autumns.

Pushing that disturbing thought aside, Libby touched Sam's arm, pointing upward to several snowy-white cattle egrets that had yet to migrate south. Sam watched in silence as the storklike birds gracefully descended to the lake and their nests.

"Aren't they lovely?" she whispered, awed, as always, by the beauty of her surroundings.

Sam nodded his agreement. Slowly he walked to the edge of the water, his eyes taking in every detail of the newly constructed dock, the fishing and paddle boats and, in the middle of the vast lake, an island gazebo, it's roof outlined with tiny white twinkle lights.

"Don't tell me, let me guess," Libby said, when he opened his mouth, apparently to tell her what he thought. "'Very nice.'"

Sam had the grace to look embarrassed. "Very nice *indeed*."

She laughed softly at the qualification. "Want to check out the gazebo? We have a paddle boat and another twenty minutes before the sun disappears behind the trees."

"Why not?" Sam agreed, much to her delight.

In no time, they had scrambled onto the boat, which resembled an oversized three-wheeler. Once seated side by side on the narrow seat, Libby and Sam both positioned their feet on the bicycle pedals mounted on the floor just in front of them. The boat soon responded to the action of their legs, shooting away from the shore. Its giant, ridged "tires" sent skyward a spray of sparkling droplets as they churned their way to the gazebo.

Fingers of sunset gold reached across the lake when they reached the octagonal structure. Solid wood halfway up and sectioned lattice the rest of the way to the roof, the gazebo was lined all around the inside with a cushioned shelf that served as seating. Sam and Libby made use of it, scrambling out of the boat to sit together in the semidarkened enclosure so they could witness the sunset.

The crickets and tree frogs had begun their nightly serenade by this time, harmonizing with a skill born of Mother Nature's direction. The spell of romance was in the air— heavy, tangible. Sam laid his arm across the ledge behind Libby and smiled warmly at her, an expression she cherished since it seemed to say he felt the wonder, too. Sympathetic to his reverence, she smiled back, snuggling up to him when he dropped his arm down to pull her close.

Libby rested her head on Sam's shoulder with a sigh of contentment. She slipped her hands around his waist, locking her fingers together. The sun dipped ever lower while they watched in companionable silence. The shadows of evening shifted, purpled and blanketed them. Chills danced up her spine and down her arms—chills that had nothing whatsoever to do with the autumn breeze.

Not surprisingly, her mind drifted back to the last time she'd been in Sam's arms and to the shivery kisses they'd shared. Those kisses had haunted her all afternoon and even now, hours later, she hungered for more. Why? she asked herself, baffled by this unexpected deviation from a lifetime of common sense. He wasn't a man she would marry, yet here she was, lost in his embrace, aching for him and questioning the philosophy of romantic love she'd followed for years.

Sam shifted his body then, turning slightly so his eyes could meet hers. Even in the dusky dark, she saw the glow in them—a glow that kindled a matching one in her own. With a soft moan of defeat, she gave in to her need, raising her face for his kiss. His lips brushed lightly over hers at first, gently fanning her smouldering desire. Impatient with that teasing caress, Libby slid her hands upward over his back to hold him tighter.

She pressed her lips to his, demanding more. He grunted in satisfaction, pulling her hard against him, crushing his lips to hers and igniting to full flame the blaze in her soul. Gasping for air, Libby tipped her head back. Sam took advantage of her breathlessness, kissing her chin, her ear, her neck.

Then he, too, had to come up for oxygen. His gasp and shuddering exhalation filled her ears and touched her heart. Libby buried her face in his neck. He rested his chin on the top of her head. Neither said a word for several mystical moments as reality gradually returned, bringing with it the black of night and the chill of autumn.

Sam released her and reached back to unclasp her hands so he could stand. Reluctantly, Libby let him go. Their eyes met; she managed a shaky smile. "Would you call *that* 'very nice'?" she asked ever-so-softly.

"I'd call that electric," Sam said, proving his point by bending swiftly down, touching his lips to hers in yet another kiss, one that set every last millimeter of her body atingle.

Dazed and disoriented when he finally raised his head again, Libby glanced out toward the mirror-smooth lake, now sprinkled with stars. She then looked heavenward, realizing with a start just how dark the sky had grown. Polaris shone brightly, flanked by Hercules, Cepheus the King and Aries the Ram—familiar constellations on which she'd gazed for years. But somehow they looked different to-night, twinkling far brighter than she'd ever seen them. *Are they in my eyes?* she wondered.

"It's getting late," Sam murmured, breaking into her trance. "We'd better get back."

She nodded her agreement, but halted his immediate move to leave with a hand on his biceps. Sam turned, one eyebrow arched in silent questioning, and then groaned when he saw the look on her face. In one smooth motion, he drew her into his arms, kissing her with savage intensity that told her victory might not be so impossible in spite of what he said—that maybe, just maybe, the magic of ro-mance had finally touched him.

Chapter Five

A good twenty minutes passed before the boat finally nudged the well-lighted dock. Libby stood up immediately.

"Wait a second," Sam said. "I need to talk to you."

"All right." Libby reached for the tie-up rope and wrapped it around one of the wooden dock supports. After greeting Fetch, tail-tapping a welcome home from his perch at the very end of the dock, she sat back down beside her boss. "I'm listening."

Sam hesitated, hating what he had to tell her. His impulsive plan to turn the tables on Libby, to prove how perilous a place like Wildwood could be, had backfired terribly. He now regretted his stupid idea and that lethal kiss in the gazebo—a kiss intended to be nothing more than a quick lesson on the pitfalls of romance. "There's something I have to know first."

"What's that?" She frowned, clearly curious.

"Have you decided to fill in for Patty tonight? Was all *that*—" he pointed to the gazebo "—to prove to me how wonderful romance can be?"

Libby laughed gaily. "Of course not. Have you forgotten what I said this afternoon? I'd never play Patty— even to save Wildwood—and *that* was definitely not on my agenda."

"I thought as much," Sam murmured, grinding to dust a clump of dirt under his foot, "I'm afraid I have a confession to make."

"A confession?" she echoed, frowning again. "What are you talking about?"

"That little interlude may not have been on your agenda, but as of forty-five minutes ago, it was on mine. That's when I, uh, decided it was time to turn the tables—to teach *you* a lesson or two."

"I don't understand," Libby said, shrinking slightly away from him.

And no wonder, Sam thought. So far he'd made a major mess of things tonight, from losing control a moment ago to his babbling explanation now. "Do you remember what I said this afternoon about Wildwood being dangerous?"

"Because it distorts reality?" Libby asked with an indulgent smile.

"Exactly."

"I remember. And I still believe you're wrong."

"Do you?" Sam drew in a deep breath and forged ahead. "What happened in the gazebo was no accident, Libby. It was a calculated attempt on my part to demonstrate how romantic surroundings can play havoc with level heads and common sense. You'd already told me that you never waste time on men you wouldn't marry. I figured if I could make you forget that I'm one of those men you would see just how hazardous a place like this can be."

As his words sank home, Libby's face began to burn. So much for Sam's being touched by the magic of romance. He was still the same ol' divorce attorney—cynical, hard and hellbent on selling Wildwood. He would never change, and in trying to make him, *she* had foolishly succumbed to the magic herself.

"Don't you think you got a little carried away?" she asked, nailing him to the seat with her eyes. "I mean, wouldn't *one* kiss have been sufficient to prove your point?"

He wouldn't meet her accusing stare, instead looking out across the lake without answering.

"Well, congratulations on a job well done, Mr. Knight," Libby snapped when the silence grew weighty. She stood. *"I get your point."* At that, she scrambled from the boat, first jogging and then running all the way to the sanctuary of her cabin, her trusty pet loping along behind.

"How humiliating," Libby wailed to Fetch, inside her living quarters not ten minutes later. The canine perked up his ears but never budged from where he lay on the bed, watching her. "Do you realize that I came *this* close—" she held up a thumb and forefinger, almost touching "—to making a place in my heart for that man when he *didn't even reserve one*?"

Libby stepped out of her pants and tossed them in the general direction of the basket-weave hamper. She tugged off both tops to send them flying, too. Unbraiding her hair as she padded barefoot to the bathroom, she then snatched up a hairbrush and bent over, using it to untangle the remains of the plait. Straightening up, Libby next vented her frustration by brushing out the resulting waves until they crackled with static electricity.

"I should have known he was up to something," she told Fetch when she walked back into the bedroom, hair floating like a veil about her face and shoulders. "Why else would a man like him show interest in a woman like me? Why, we're different as daylight and dark, and to think I stood out there, kissing him as if he might be the knight I've saved myself for all these years."

She plopped down on the bed. "Not that he's not knight material, you understand. Deep down inside, he is, and I suspect that's what attracts me to him. Unfortunately, I'm waiting for a Lancelot or a Galahad. He's definitely an Arthur—too work oriented, too level-headed, too grim." She sighed. "He's also too darned sneaky."

Fetch's accusing brown stare never wavered.

"Okay, okay, I admit it," Libby said, somewhat defensively. "I probably deserved what he did to me. I almost turned him over to Patty for the same treatment, after all. And, just between you and me, he's right about the effect romantic surroundings can have on a couple or—" she winced "—a fanciful female like me. But what he doesn't seem to understand is that the men and women who come here are married—*already committed*—when they arrive. They need the romance to survive."

Libby reached out, absently petting her dog, and sighed. "I guess it's all over, sport. Sam's going to sell Wildwood. Nine people will hit the unemployment lines and all my dreams to manage a resort like this, all my hard work, will go up in smoke."

Fetch licked her hand and whined softly, a sound lost when the phone beside the bed jingled intrusively. Libby reached for it.

"Hello," she said, as she lay back to prop her head on her dog's back and her feet on the brass headboard.

"Hi, there!" Ramona's bubbly voice came over the line. "How's it going?"

"Fine," Libby lied.

"Ever come up with a Plan C?"

"As a matter of fact, yes," Libby hedged, unwilling to share all the depressing details of her day with this old friend who would never, ever let her forget them. "I confronted Sam straight out about selling Wildwood, and he agreed to give me the rest of the weekend to convince him not to."

"You're kidding!" Ramona exclaimed, obviously astounded.

"No, I'm not. So far we've toured the pool, the sauna, one of the cabins—"

"Was he properly impressed?"

"Of course," Libby told her, thinking that "very nice" could possibly translate into "properly impressed."

"Sounds like you've got everything under control," Ramona said enthusiastically. "I knew you had it in you!"

"Yes, well..."

"What's up next? Dinner?"

"Actually we—"

"Great! Have your mother make him some of that marvelous shrimp gumbo of hers. He'll love it."

"Mona, I—"

"And why don't you take him for a moonlight stroll by the lake after that? There's not a soul alive who's immune to one of those."

Libby nearly swallowed her tongue and quickly abandoned further attempts to come clean. "I'll think about it."

"Wear the teal silk outfit with the scarf I gave you last Christmas and keep me posted, okay?"

"Okay," Libby promised automatically, seconds later dropping the receiver into the cradle. She covered her eyes with her hands, groaning loudly. "Elizabeth Ann Turner, you are gutless!"

Why hadn't she just told Ramona the truth—admitted that she was no match for the likes of Sam Knight, that more than the fate of Wildwood was now at stake? But no. If Libby revealed the chaotic state of her heart, Sam's sister would be at Wildwood before morning to check things out. Of those two evils, a weekend with Sam was definitely the lesser.

Wasn't it...?

Libby shook her head in wonder. How had she ever gotten into such a fix? More importantly how was she going to get out of it? If she pretended that nothing had ever happened—that they hadn't kissed like lovers in the gazebo—would their relationship be strictly business again? Probably, she told herself. Sam had made perfectly clear *his* motives for their romantic encounters thus far. He would be more than willing to do his part.

But what about me? Libby agonized, painfully reminded of her unpredictable conduct of late. Sam intrigued her as no other man had, and she responded accordingly. Thank goodness he thought her wanton behavior to be the result of his carefully planned seduction.

Encouraged by that thought, Libby decided to give changing Sam's mind just one more try. She crawled out of bed and walked to the closet, folding back the louvered doors to scan her wardrobe. Remembering what Ramona had suggested, Libby pulled out the two-piece dress she'd bought for her friend's recent wedding. Scandalously expensive, the versatile skirt and blouse could be worn many ways and dressed up or down.

Deciding up was definitely in order tonight. Libby gathered together black lingerie, an ornate gold belt and the scarf Ramona had mentioned. Tossing them onto the bed, she headed to the bathroom and the hot tub she hoped would restore her body and spirit.

Nearly an hour later, Libby stepped out onto her porch, fully dressed and definitely renewed—in body, at least.

Making one last attempt to brighten the hue of her blue mood, she glanced down at the knotted scarf she wore, straightening it for the umpteenth time. She then secured the tortoise shell combs she'd used to sweep back her mass of sable hair and, assured she looked the part of a sensible young businesswoman, headed to Sam's lighted cabin.

With every step, Libby's full skirt swirled around her legs, as sensuous as moonlit water on bare flesh. The fragrance of roses caressed her face and hair, capturing her low-flying spirits in a scented updraft that sent them soaring back to their usual lofty heights. Squaring her shoulders with new determination, Libby stepped onto Sam's porch, knocked firmly on the door and waited. Almost immediately, bright light flooded the veranda. *Keep your cool,* Libby reminded herself just as the door flew open and she found her eyes level with a broad bare chest.

Her cool self-destructed.

"I, uh, hi there," she blurted. "Ready?"

"For what?" Sam asked, his gaze missing not one detail of Libby's hair, loose and touchable for a change, or her dress, perfectly elegant. His recent resolution to avoid her the rest of the weekend—a result of over an hour's worth of soul-searching and goal reaffirmation—sailed right up the chimney.

"Dinner at seven."

"We're still on?" he asked, wondering if his worst fears were now truth. Had Libby seen through him? Did she know how close he'd come to surrender in the gazebo? Was this dinner à deux an attempt to finish him off for good?

"Of course," she told him with a dazzling smile. "If you still want to, that is."

"That depends on whether or not you've found your temper," Sam hedged, hoping she might reveal the reason for this disconcerting about-face.

"It's found, all right," she assured him. "And under lock and key. I'm sorry I ever lost it in the first place. I had no right. I wasn't above deception myself, to prove a point."

"In that case, I'd love to have dinner with you," Sam said, relief washing over him. From all appearances, Libby believed his explanation of what had happened between them. A platonic dinner together tonight would reinforce his story. Sam looked down at his sweats, threadbare and clinging to skin still damp from the bath he'd just taken. "I'll have to change first . . ."

"Take your time," Libby said. "I'll wait right out here on the porch swing."

Barely twenty minutes later, Sam joined Libby. Together they walked to the restaurant, tastefully illuminated with gaslights and quite popular, judging from the number of cars parked in front of it.

"Do a lot of the locals dine up here?" he asked, surprised by the turnout.

"Uh-huh," Libby told him with a nod. "Especially on the weekends. We have some regulars from as far away as Little Rock, too. My mom has been in the gourmet-restaurant business for years. She has her own recipes and has even published a cookbook. I always mention her name as chef when I advertise."

"Am I dressed okay for this?" Sam asked, glancing down at his leather sport coat and the coordinating pants he'd retrieved from over the shower curtain rod only a short time before. They'd dried relatively wrinkle free, but were far from formal by anyone's standards.

Libby laughed. "You ate there in jeans this morning, remember? And though we're a little more 'propah' in the evenings—" she lifted to her mouth an imaginary teacup, her pinky delicately extended "—you could still ditch that tie and get away with it."

Realizing he must have tugged that hated silken hangman's noose one time too many, Sam grinned his thanks and set to work ridding himself of it. Libby took the tie, folded it neatly and stashed it in his jacket pocket for him. A second later, top button of his pale blue shirt unfastened, Sam sucked in his first adequate supply of air since dressing.

A middle-aged woman met the two of them at the door of the restaurant, and, menus in hand, escorted them to a section that Sam hadn't noticed that morning. Faceted glass from ceiling to floor on two sides, the dimly lit room was easily the most romantic in the house, a fact not lost on Sam, who experienced a sudden resurgence of doubt about Libby's motives for this dinner. *Did* she suspect the truth about his weakness for her after all? Was she out for revenge?

"Would you rather sit somewhere else?" she asked, as though reading his thoughts. "Mrs. Carter knows this is my favorite table and assumed—"

"This is fine," he interjected, somewhat reassured and determined she wouldn't find out how very susceptible he really was.

He helped Libby with her chair and then sat opposite her at the cozy table. Flaming tapers illuminated their corner, a glow reflected in the china, crystal and silver artfully arranged on the snowy linen tablecloth. The roughly hewn log wall on one side of the room and the hardwood floor beneath their feet contrasted sharply with the elegant table, contributing to the rustic beauty that spelled pure romance.

Sam wasn't unaffected by the charm. His gaze found Libby across the table. He noted that her nutmeg eyes had received more than their fair share of the candlelight and now twinkled attractively. He could smell her perfume from where he sat, a scent that reminded him of flowers in the springtime. She caught his eye and smiled. His heart turned a somersault.

"What would you like to drink?" asked a young waitress, who'd materialized from nowhere. Sam barely registered her words.

"I'll have iced tea, please," Libby said, looking expectantly his way.

"Uh, me, too," he murmured, mustering up just enough sense to realize he was in no fit state to handle anything stronger.

When the waitress left them, Libby opened her menu. "I'm so hungry. What are you going to eat?"

"What do you recommend?" Sam countered, not sure his glazed eyes would focus on the menu.

"I was thinking about shrimp gumbo. My mom makes the best in the world."

Sam snapped right out of his stupor. He picked up his own menu, quickly scanning it and spotting the entrée she mentioned. "I'll have that, too."

"It's Cajun spicy," Libby warned.

"Perfect," he replied, nearly back to sanity. Her next words finished the job.

"Tell me something about your work, Sam. Do you handle any cases besides divorces?" She'd pushed the menu aside and propped her elbow on the table and her chin in her hand.

"When I help out one of my partners," he told her, now stone sober. He took a sip of the cool drink the waitress had just brought. The young woman, dressed in a black uniform trimmed with a lacy white collar and cuffs, took their dinner orders and left them again.

"How many partners do you have?" Libby next asked.

"Three. We each have a specialty."

"Are any of your partners married?"

"All of them," Sam told her, wondering at the line of questioning.

"Happily?"

So she'd climbed back on her soap box. Good. Their verbal fencing kept his mind on his business and beat hands down a night of sitting alone in his cabin. "At times."

"So you admit there are some successful marriages?"

"If you recall, I admitted that this afternoon."

"Just checking," she said with a laugh that begged for company.

He couldn't resist the invitation. Once again his eyes over swept her, missing not one fascinating millimeter of the woman who was Libby Turner. Once again he wondered what it was about her he found so damned desirable. He wasn't sure, but knew full well that if given the slightest encouragement, he wouldn't hesitate to whisk her away to his cabin and make slow, sweet love with her until dawn.

But would that be long enough to get her out of my system? he suddenly wondered. He knew it wouldn't. A lifetime of Libby might not be enough, and that scared the appetite right out of him.

"Mmm," Libby sighed at that moment, moving her arm so the waitress could place the gumbo in front of her. She sniffed the steam of the savory concoction, served in its bowl of hollowed-out homemade bread. "You're going to love this." She picked up her spoon and took a big bite, immediately snatching up her glass with her free hand.

"Hot?" Sam asked.

Libby nodded and hastily gulped down a swallow of the soothing liquid.

"Pepper or fire?"

"Both," she promised. Sam chuckled at her reply, a sexy sound that only served to heighten her incredible awareness of him. From the moment she'd found herself face to chest with him not so very long ago, her professionalism had eluded her. So much for keeping things platonic, she thought with a mental sigh. As long as there was any chance Sam might be the knight of her dreams, she could kiss her usual level-headedness goodbye.

Sam? The knight of her dreams? Libby stared into her gumbo, wondering if he could, indeed be the one. His mail was a tad tarnished, but then the shine of the armor wasn't nearly as important as the man underneath it all.

How will I ever be sure it's him? she then wondered, raising her gaze to the possible cavalier sitting across the table from her. He toyed with his food, managing a half a bite, and then looked up to intercept her stare. He didn't speak, but Libby saw in his cobalt eyes a gleam that had nothing to do with the candle flickering between them. She realized with a start that contrary to what he'd led her to believe that afternoon, he would be a more-than-willing participant in a test for knighthood.

And then what? she asked herself, knowing if the test results were positive he would never be interested in more than a short-term relationship. Was that what she wanted from him? She suspected it wasn't, and that scared the appetite right out of her.

Libby pushed the bowl away murmuring, "I guess I'm not as hungry as I thought."

"Me, either," Sam said.

"Dessert?"

"No thanks."

An awkward silence followed his words. Then they both spoke at once. Laughing softly, Sam yielded the floor.

"I know it's early yet," Libby said. "But I have some paper work I need to take care of tonight. Would you mind if we...?"

"Not at all," Sam told her, visibly relieved. So he was uncomfortable, too, Libby realized. Suspecting why, and afraid to find out for sure, she got to her feet.

"Dinner was on the house," she teased, in an effort to lighten the mood.

Sam grinned at the irony of that and stood, fishing in his pocket for the tip, which he left on the table. Taking Libby's elbow, he guided her to the kitchen and the chef, busy behind the scenes. After complimenting Mrs, Turner, Libby's very youthful mother, he led the way out the back exit, headed to Libby's apartment at the other end of the building.

"Does the noise next door ever keep you awake at night?" he asked as they walked through the dew-kissed grass.

"Nothing keeps *me* awake at night," she assured him with a light laugh, climbing the steps to her back door.

"Nothing?" he echoed.

"Nothing."

Certain he could prove her wrong if given half a chance, Sam joined her there on the porch. She stood kissably close, but he resisted temptation, remembering vividly the near disaster in the gazebo.

"Goodnight, Sam," Libby whispered, her eyes on his mouth.

"Goodnight," he replied, his on hers. He turned, actually managing one step away before he muttered, "Oh, what the hell?" and spun around to enfold her in his arms.

They kissed with a hunger born of forbidden desire, bodies pressed tightly together, hearts racing. With a groan, Sam stumbled to the porch swing, dragging her with him.

Pulling her down on his lap, he covered her lips with his again.

Libby willingly opened her mouth to his questing tongue. Her own circled his, at first tentatively and then with an urgency that matched his. Sam moved his hands skillfully over her arms and then back, demanding yet soothing, through the thin fabric of her blouse. Libby trailed her mouth over his jawline and chin, breathing deeply of the scent that was so distinctly Sam. Reaching out, she unbuttoned three more buttons of his shirt and then nuzzled her face to the bare flesh over his hammering heart, reveling in the tickle of the coarse hairs sprinkled there.

Sam caught his breath, abandoning his sensual massage of her back to brush his fingertips over one of her breasts. When she moaned softly in response, he cupped his hand around the fullness, teasing the hardened tip with his thumb.

Libby sagged weakly against him, overcome with an aching need as intense as it was new to her. She knew she should stop Sam, but caught up in the excitement of his feverish kisses, she hadn't the will—or strength—to do it.

Luckily, Fetch had both. Clearly jealous of the man sitting in *his* spot on the swing, the big black canine revealed his displeasure by whining a complaint. When that produced no results, he clamped his teeth none-too-gently around Sam's jacket sleeve, growling menacingly as he dragged the man's hand away from Libby's blouse.

"Fetch Turner!" Libby exclaimed, aghast, pushing her pet away.

Sam hooted at that, laughing so hard the swing shook. Baffled by his unexpected behavior, Libby glared at him, and then, when that didn't work, put her hands on his shoulders to give him a straighten-up-right-now shake.

"Just what is so darned funny?" she demanded.

"Fetch *Turner*?" he managed to blurt between gasps for air.

Libby bristled. "He *is* a member of my family."

"Right," Sam murmured dryly, wiping his eyes with the back of his hand.

Neither moved for a moment. Every nerve ending in Libby's body served as radar, finely attuned to Sam, and when his mood swung from amusement back to desire she responded accordingly. Libby raised her face, nuzzling his chin with her lips.

"No," he said to her astonishment, setting her firmly off his lap and on the other end of the swing.

"But—"

"Fetch just saved your virtue, darling, and if you don't want him to spend the night on the porch because some loco lawyer has stolen his place in your bed, I suggest you stay right there."

That sobered her.

A long, awkward silence ensued. Libby chewed her bottom lip. Fetch watched her with doleful eyes. Sam restlessly shifted his position once and then twice, bobbling the swing and finally setting it in brisk motion with a firm nudge of his foot on the wooden floor.

"What's wrong?" Libby demanded, grabbing the arm rest to keep from falling out.

"Nothing!" he snapped.

"Are you angry at me?"

"Of course not."

"At Fetch?"

"No, he was just doing his job."

"Then what's the matter?"

"I told you. Nothing."

There was another heavy silence. Tension as tangible as lightning, arced between them.

"You don't feel well, do you?" Libby blurted, unable to tolerate the suspense a moment longer. "The gumbo didn't sit well and you won't admit it."

"The gumbo was fine," he replied rather impatiently.

"Would a cold drink help?" she persisted.

"Not unless I shower in it!" he snarled.

"Oh," Libby blushed furiously, finally getting the picture. Clearly her boss was in as bad a shape as she. "Sam?"

"What?"

"Did you...? Was that...?" She sighed. "Were you trying to prove another point when you kissed me just now?"

"Hell, no," he told her, a second later adding rather uncertainly, "Were you?"

"Hell, no," she mimicked.

"Then why are we sitting here, like a couple of lovesick teenagers, dying to go in and finish what we started?"

"Beats me," Libby murmured glumly. "We both know we have nothing in common but this resort."

"You can say that again."

"And we know we're opposites."

"Exactly."

"And we know that I never, ever waste my precious time on any man I wouldn't marry."

"Right," he agreed with a solemn nod.

"So why can't I resist you?" Libby exploded in exasperation.

"You can't resist me?"

"No."

"Good," Sam responded. "Because I can't resist you, either."

"You can't?"

He shook his head.

Libby groaned. "What is the matter with us? Why are we acting like this?"

"Because we can't help it," Sam told her, halting the swing and getting abruptly to his feet. "Come on, I'll show you what's to blame for this insanity." He reached down to help Libby up and then guided her to the edge of the porch. Pointing heavenward, he drew her attention to the full moon, shining brightly down on them.

"The moon?" she questioned, confused.

"The moon, the flowers, the lake, the autumn wind and everything else at your honeymoon hideaway. This place is lethal. We aren't right for one another, yet here we stand, nearly lovers... Can't you see the danger?"

Libby winced at his candid words. "I see the danger...to a man and woman like us, anyway."

"Well thank the Lord for small favors," Sam muttered, visibly relieved. "It's just as I told you before—a resort like Wildwood can mess up your mind. All this—" he swept his arm, including the whole resort "—makes living together seem so desirable, so easy. You've created a dream world here, Libby, one that perpetrates the happily-ever-after theory of life. And though your intentions are good, in doing so, you actually hinder the married couples who visit by destroying their ability to cope with reality."

Libby held her tongue until he stopped to breathe when she put a finger to his lips. "Did you hear what you just said?"

"Of course I heard what I just said," he retorted, capturing that offending finger in his hand. "I said it."

"Then you do realize that the men and women who come here are married?"

"Now that would be pretty darn hard to prove...unless you ask to see a marriage license when they check in," Sam grumbled.

"True," Libby conceded. "And I don't require a license, but I think I'd be fairly safe in saying that fifty percent of them are legal anyway."

"Probably more," he grudgingly admitted, "if the graffiti on the cars is anything to go by."

"I agree. And since the couples who come here are already committed to one another, the danger, as you put it, of Wildwood is neutralized. It performs its intended function, providing a haven from all those problems you mentioned."

"A pit stop in the rat race of life?" Sam dryly interjected.

"I'm serious!" Libby snapped, not for the first time losing her patience with him.

Sam pulled her into his arms, resting his chin on her head. "I know you are, and if it'll make you feel any better, the lawyer in me has to admit that you're making some sense."

"Are you actually admitting there might be a grain of truth in what I've said?" Libby asked, tipping her head back to look him dead in the eye.

"Yes, I am—God help me."

She smiled, pleased by that unexpected victory. "Does that mean you've changed your mind about getting rid of Wildwood?"

"Not on your life. Come Monday, Ramona is going to call the representatives of those two franchises, and if either one of them is still interested, I'm out."

Libby eased free of his embrace. "Then I'd better get to work," she said, moving determinedly toward the door. "You're mine until Monday, and I've got to line up a few ghosts."

"Ghosts?" Sam asked with an incredulous laugh.

"Ghosts," she told him with a firm nod. She whistled to Fetch, followed her pet inside and shut the door behind her without another word.

Shaking his head in bemusement, Sam stepped off her porch, walking with reluctant steps to his distressingly empty, oh-so-lonely cabin.

Chapter Six

Libby dragged herself out of bed just before the sun rose Sunday morning, not an easy feat since something—or maybe someone—had cost her a sleepless night. Rueing the fact that she hadn't knocked on wood when bragging that nothing ever kept her awake, Libby dressed in beat-up sneakers, faded jeans and a sweatshirt sporting a picture of a female angler and the legend, Support Your Local Hooker. Fifteen minutes after her feet hit the floor, she stepped out her door, fully equipped with a thermos of coffee, a sack of pastries stolen from the kitchen and a well-planned strategy.

Fetch bounded out with her, his long black tail wagging his delight at the early outing. Snatching up a tackle box and two of the fishing rods she kept handy on a rack just outside the door, Libby made her way carefully down the steps. Fetch, who knew this morning routine well, sailed right off the porch and loped toward the small lake. He halted in confusion seconds later when Libby whistled at him and, whirling, caught up with her as she crossed the road and walked to Sam's cabin.

Juggling her unwieldy load, Libby managed a peek at her watch, noting it was just before seven. She sniffed the air, smiling with pleasure at the mingled scents she inhaled— roses, dew-moistened pine, juniper.... How she loved her mountain, especially early like this, just as the black of night dawned into the bright of day. Humming to herself, she climbed the steps of unit six. She didn't hesitate, but walked straight to Sam's door and, after shifting all her burden to one arm, knocked on it. When no one answered immediately, she knocked again, louder. Still there was no response.

Libby frowned. Had Sam had second thoughts about giving her his weekend? she suddenly wondered, her heart skipping a beat at the very thought. Had he slipped away in the night and gone back to Memphis...*before* she'd changed his mind? Libby dumped the food and gear on the porch and did her best to find out.

"Sam!" she called through the door, banging on it with both fists, "Wake up!"

She heard a muffled "Goway," and, overwhelmed with relief that she still had her reluctant guest, sagged against the wooden barrier.

Go away, huh? Libby grinned. Fat chance. She'd spent the major portion of the night before planning the rest of Sam's weekend. She was committed now, and nothing short of disaster would sway her from her goal.

Impishly, Libby dug out the keys she'd stashed in her pocket only moments before. She inserted the Master into Sam's lock and then turned the knob to quietly open the door. Libby's eyes, well adjusted to the semidark by this time, located Sam immediately. Sprawled facedown on the bed in nothing but briefs, he lay with one leg and arm under the blanket and his head buried beneath two pillows.

After hanging back for half a second, Libby got up the nerve to approach the bed, for a short moment toying with the idea of kissing him awake. She abandoned that foolhardy notion almost immediately, however. She knew her limits but *didn't* know Sam's. One husky "Morning" might be all it would take to send them both over the edge...or between the sheets.

"Sic 'im, Fetch," she whispered to her dog instead. Gleefully, the canine leapt onto the bed and the unsuspecting male sleeping so peacefully. A second later, a very cold nose and an eager pink tongue found the small of Sam's bare back.

"Arrrgh!" Her boss rolled off the bed to land in a tangle of pillows, blankets and long, muscled legs at Libby's feet.

Sadist that she was, Libby howled with laughter, a sound that turned into a screech of surprise when Sam grabbed for her ankles and yanked her feet right out from under her. She fell heavily on the bed. Sam rose to his knees, mercilessly dragging her—squealing and clutching at the sheet—into his waiting arms. He then fell back on the heap of bed linens on the floor, taking her with him.

"You rat!" Libby exclaimed, laughing as she struggled to free herself. But she couldn't, and a twist of Sam's body put her fully beneath him, hands pinned between them. Their eyes met. Her laughter died.

Sam, who hadn't said a word, smiled lazily at Libby and lowered his face with slow deliberation. Her lips tingled with anticipation of his kiss—a kiss that never came. Instead he nuzzled her neck with his whisker-roughened face and teased her earlobe with his lips and tongue.

Libby melted into a puddle of submission beneath him.

Chuckling softly, Sam shifted his weight onto his forearms, a move that freed her hands. He tangled his fingers in her disheveled hair and then, as though reading her secret desires, gave her the kiss she craved. Intensely aware of every bare inch of him, Libby abandoned her token resistance, wrapping her arms tightly around his neck, returning that kiss with enthusiasm ... until Fetch decided he wanted to play, too. With a yelp of joy, the massive canine pounced.

"Damn dumb dog!" Sam exploded, ducking his head to avoid Fetch's ever-ready tongue. "It's no wonder you're not married with that flop-eared mutt acting as chaperon."

"Fetch is not dumb!" Libby retorted hotly, pushing her boss and her dog away so she could scramble to her feet. Resisting the urge to physically defend her pet, Libby put her hands on her hips and glared down at Sam. "He just wants us to quit fooling around so we can get on with this."

"How can we 'get on with this' if we quit fooling around?" Sam demanded, glaring right back at her from where he lay on the floor.

Puffing her irritation at getting sidetracked from her goal, Libby stalked to the door and reached outside to retrieve the fishing rods. She held them up for Sam to see. "Not that—*this*. Contrary to what you obviously think, I did not come here to—" She broke off. Suddenly intensely aware of Sam's near nakedness and exactly what she would like to do about it, she turned her back on him and blurted, "I came to take you fishing."

"Well why didn't you say so?" Sam demanded instantly, Libby's duenna dog now the last thing on his mind. He leaped to his feet, snatching up a pair of jeans from his open bag. As soon as he tugged them on, he dug around for a shirt, which he quickly pulled over his head. He didn't take the time for socks, however, sticking his bare feet right into the leather deck shoes. "Okay. I'm decent."

Libby turned rather cautiously. "All set?" she asked.

"Just as soon as I find my glasses," he told her, perusing the bedside table. He found them on the floor beside it, put them on, laughing softly when the blurry letters on her sweatshirt cleared and divided themselves into words.

"What's so funny?" Libby demanded.

"Support Your Local Hooker?"

She glanced down at the bright red letters and grinned. "A present from my dad last birthday. Like it?"

"It's, uh, colorful," he said, teasingly adding. "And the point is well taken. Tell your dad I'd willingly do my part if that dog of yours would just let me."

Libby laughed. "My dad is six-foot-four and weighs two-seventy-one. He bought Fetch to guard the place. Still want me to tell him?"

"On second thought, better save it," Sam said with a rueful grimace as he led the way out the door.

The walk to the water took only minutes. Under Fetch's watchful eye, Libby and Sam maneuvered the flat-bottomed boat over to the dock so the three of them could climb aboard. Libby sat with her pet on the back seat of the vessel, within easy reach of the outboard motor. To keep their weight in the rear half of the boat, Sam took the middle seat, thus expediting the trip across the lake.

"I know some great spots," he offered, looking out over the sunrise-tinted water. He remembered the last time he'd gone fishing here—so many months ago—and how good it had felt to know the lake belonged to him and his heirs.

Heirs? What heirs? Sam Knight had no heirs and never would have since he didn't want to take another chance on the wife required to sire them. Oh, it wasn't that he didn't like children. He did . . . a lot, in fact. But as far as he was concerned, marriage was too high a price to pay for a couple of offspring, especially when the likelihood of divorce was so great. He'd come from a broken home, himself, and wouldn't wish so unstable an upbringing on any kid.

Now if things were different—if Libby were right and two people really could live happily together, marriage might not be so bad. There were definitely some benefits to that institution, like having someone share the bad times, someone to bring the good, someone to laugh with, talk with, play with . . . someone to love.

Sometimes—like last night—Sam needed someone to love.

So buy yourself a parakeet, he thought, at once disgusted with the maudlin direction his thoughts had taken. Obviously Wildwood had gotten under his skin, opening old wounds, resurrecting old dreams—just as he'd feared it would. And that, of course, explained his sleepless night and the heaviness in his heart. Well, it was time to get hold of himself. Contrary to what Ms. Libby Turner believed, forever-after unions only happened in fairy tales. Sam preferred nonfiction.

"I guess I should warn you we won't be alone this morning," Libby said from behind him. Her words barely dented Sam's abstraction.

"Hmm?"

"We're going to have company," she repeated, adding. "Are you awake?"

"Of course I am," Sam retorted, getting a grip on himself with difficulty. He glanced at the plastic thermos laying on the floor at his feet. "Is that coffee you brought?"

"Uh-huh."

"Mind if I . . . ?"

"Help yourself."

While Libby cranked the motor, Sam reached for the thermos and the hot brew he hoped would dissolve his stupor. He poured some into the flat-bottomed lid, took a big swallow and tensed, suddenly registering what Libby had said a moment before about having company. Sam turned, intending to demand an explanation, but gave up that idea immediately. The motor had sputtered into life by now. She would never hear him over the roar. Knowing he would find his coffee in his face if he didn't drink it before take off, Sam gulped the last stimulating drops and put the lid back on the thermos. At that moment, Libby put the boat in motion, sending them flying over the lake.

The front of the boat tipped up as they accelerated, barely skimming the water. Frosty morning air ripped by Sam, tugging his clothes. Totally revived now, he glanced back at Libby. One hand on the steering throttle, the other holding her hair back out of her eyes, she concentrated on guiding the speeding boat. Her face positively glowed, and Sam grinned, pleased that she seemed to be enjoying the outing as much as he. Not that many women—at least not the ones he dealt with these days—liked angling. Libby handled the boat like a pro and was clearly the exception.

To his surprise, she didn't head to any of the fishing holes he knew, instead directing the craft to a small inlet not visible from the rest of the resort. There, nestled deep in the woods, sat the old log cabin Sam had asked about on Friday night. Left over from frontier days, it had obviously been remodeled, but it was still a vision of rustic beauty. He wouldn't have been surprised to see Daniel Boone standing at the door.

But it wasn't Daniel who stepped out of the structure when Libby killed the motor and let the boat bump to a halt against the rocky shoreline. It was Santa Claus ... or a very reasonable facsimile. Dressed in denim overalls and a bright red flannel shirt, the bearded bear of a man raised an arm to wave a greeting.

Libby yelled back an enthusiastic, "Ahoy there!" She got to her feet, stepping carefully over the tackle box and snatching up the sack as she made her way to the front of the boat. When she got even with Sam, he stood and turned, effectively blocking her path.

"Who's that?" he demanded, looking back over his shoulder toward the rotund gentleman fast approaching.

"Why, one of the Ghosts of Marriage Past, of course," she told him, slipping by to scramble out the front of the boat. Fetch didn't waste a moment, either, leaping right over the side and into the water. He splashed his way to dry land, where he shook himself off. Stunned by Libby's revelation, Sam moved much more slowly, not quite sure what to make of the white-haired old man who'd now caught Libby up in a king-size hug.

At that moment, a plump, gray-haired woman who could only be Mrs. Claus—or was it Mrs. Ghost?—appeared at the corner of the cabin, stopping short when she spied the three of them. Her rosy cheeks rounded even more when she smiled. She, too, waved and hurried lakeside.

"Sam," Libby said, laying her free hand on his arm. "These are my grandparents, Edwin and Martha Turner. Mamaw, Papaw, this is the owner of Wildwood, Sam Knight."

"It's a real pleasure," Edwin said, grasping Sam's hand in an iron grip and pumping it vigorously.

Still trying to assimilate what was happening, Sam barely managed to nod civilly in reply.

"You said you'd be here by seven-fifteen," Martha fussed, hugging Libby to her ample bosom even as her dark eyes appraised Sam from head to toe. "We'd almost given you two up."

"Sorry," Libby told her, easing free. She looked pointedly at Sam. "We had a little...complication."

He nearly choked. *Little* complication? That put it mildly. His life would never be the same. "You two are ghosts, er, *guests* here?" he blurted to change the subject.

"We're celebrating our fiftieth wedding anniversary," Martha Turner told him proudly, tucking her arm through her husband's. "This weekend at Wildwood is a gift from our grandchildren."

Sam's jaw dropped. "Did you say *fiftieth*?"

"That's right," Edwin said, beaming. "Fifty years ago today, me and the prettiest little miss in Arkansas slipped over the state line and tied the knot."

"I was about Libby's size then," Martha explained with a warm laugh.

"Fifty years," Sam muttered, shaking his head. "But you two look so young."

"I'm sixty-nine," Edwin volunteered. "Got married when I was nineteen. Martha, here, was only sixteen."

"And you've stayed together all these years," the younger man mused aloud. "That's incredible."

"Sam's a lawyer," Libby explained to her grandparents. "A *divorce* lawyer. He spends most of his time in court and doesn't believe in love and marriage anymore."

"Doesn't believe in love?" Martha exclaimed aghast.

"Or marriage?" Edwin added in disbelief. The two of them exchanged a glance and then looked at Sam as though he might be from another planet.

"Nope," Libby replied oh-so-casually, ignoring her boss's glare of warning. "I thought you two might be a refreshing change for him."

"I should say," her grandmother murmured.

Edwin slapped Sam on the back, nearly knocking him off his feet. "Are you hungry, son? Martha's got homemade biscuits and Petit Jean ham waiting on the picnic table over there."

"And I've got breakfast rolls," Libby added, holding up her sack.

"But what about our fishing trip?" Sam asked, glancing longingly toward the lake . . . and escape from these charming ghosts. Like another Scrooge, he wasn't so sure he wanted to learn what they had to teach.

"All in good time," Libby replied. "All in good time."

The sun topped the trees in the east and chased the morning fog clean away before the four of them finished their leisurely breakfast. Sam, who watched the older couple closely all through the meal, took note of how they acted toward each other—so respectful, so in love—and after fifty years of living under the same roof. He found that phenomena enviable and downright mindboggling, especially in light of his own, and his parents' disastrous marriages. He half wondered if Libby might have put her grandparents up to the loving display.

Vowing to find out the truth, he glanced at his watch very deliberately and got to his feet. "Eight-thirty. If we wait much longer, we won't catch a thing."

Edwin stood, too. "Got a rod?"

"I brought both of us one," Libby replied.

She yawned, throwing her arms up in a lazy stretch that tightened her sweatshirt, and the suggestion on it, over her full breasts. Intensely aware of her, as always, Sam had to look toward the woods to keep his thoughts in line.

"If it's all the same to you guys," she then said. "I think I'll stay here and keep Mamaw and Fetch company."

"That's fine with me," Sam said. Not only did he need some time away from Libby, he wanted to be alone with her spry grandfather.

Edwin nodded his agreement. He gathered up his own rod and tackle box from the cabin and, minutes later, joined

Sam where he waited in the boat. Eight-forty-five found the two of them drifting down the west bank of the lake, casting and then reeling in the crank baits they hoped would lure a keeper bass.

"Mr. Turner?" Sam asked very casually, checking out the bait he'd just freed from a sunken log.

"Call me Edwin," the man replied with a smile, casting his rod with an expert flick of the wrist.

"All right, I want to ask you something, and I want you to be honest with me when you answer."

"Sure," Edwin agreed easily. He never shifted his eyes from his fishing line and the bait now bobbing its way back to the boat.

"Do you ever regret getting married so young—spending your whole life with just one woman?"

"Nope."

"And there's nothing you'd change if you could do it all again?" Sam persisted.

"Nothing, but..." The man's voice trailed off into silence. He stopped reeling in the line and glanced uneasily toward the two women still sitting at the picnic table.

"But what?" Sam prompted softly, certain Edwin was going to admit that his marriage might not be so perfect after all.

"Well, I've been with Martha since my teens—"

"And you wish you'd sowed a few wild oats before you got married?" Sam interjected hopefully.

Edwin threw back his head, laughing heartily. "Hell, no. That woman and I sowed our wild oats together—and had a damned good time doing it." Again he glanced toward his wife and granddaughter. His smile slowly faded. "You won't repeat this?"

Sam shook his head, now very curious.

"Martha had a bout with pneumonia last winter—almost died. Seems like she's gone down some since then, and I can't help but worry about her passing on before I do." His dark eyes met Sam's. "I guess this may sound selfish, but I want to go first. I don't think I can live without her."

Touched to the heart by that reluctant confession, Sam blinked to clear his suddenly blurred vision. *So this is love* he thought, awed. Real love. The kind Libby wanted. Well, he didn't much blame her for waiting now—almost wished he were the kind of man who could give it to her. But he wasn't. Few mortal men could ever fulfill her unrealistic expectations, and *he* with his scars, was especially inadequate. All of a sudden, that bothered him.

"Your wife looks like the picture of health to me, Mr., uh, Edwin."

"Do you really think so?" the white-haired gentleman asked, frowning worriedly.

"Yes, sir, I do. I should be so fit at sixty-six."

Edwin nodded solemnly, as though somewhat reassured. "We walk two miles every day, you know—to keep fit."

"That's more than I do," Sam admitted. "And I wouldn't be surprised if you live to be a hundred…both of you."

Edwin smiled slowly and opened his mouth as though to speak, immediately abandoning that when his line went taut. The next few minutes were filled with splashes, curses and laughter as Libby's grandfather landed one of the biggest bass Sam had ever seen. Inspired by the sight of the beautifully marked fish, Sam turned his full attention to the sport he loved best. They spent three relaxing hours in the boat before Libby finally got their attention and coaxed them back to the cabin.

Edwin, displaying the four fish he'd kept on the stringer, invited Sam and Libby to stay for a lunchtime meal of fried bass.

"We can't," Libby quickly replied before Sam could get his own "We'd love to" out. "We have another luncheon engagement."

Sam flicked her a look of surprise, but held his tongue. They said their goodbyes, walking back alone to the boat, where Sam caught her arm and whispered. "What luncheon engagement?"

"We're meeting the Ghosts of Marriage Present in the restaurant at noon," Libby told him. Ignoring his immediate groan of protest she whistled for the pet who'd long since grown weary of sitting at the picnic table.

Fetch bounded from the woods and whatever mischief he'd been in, joining them with a leap that almost flipped the craft. Sam, clearly not pleased by Libby's announcement, wouldn't allow her to pilot the boat on the trip back. Humoring him, she sat on the middle seat so he could do the honors.

When they nudged to a halt at the dock a short time later, Libby and Fetch climbed quickly out of the boat. She glanced at her watch. "It's twenty minutes until noon. We have just enough time to clean up before lunch."

"Hold it," Sam ordered, joining her on the weathered wooden planks. "I have something to say to you first."

Libby turned toward him rather hesitantly, not quite sure what to expect. Had one set of ghosts been enough for him? Was he now a changed man, ready to keep Wildwood, maybe even ready to give romance a try himself? Or was he tired of her "agenda"—wanting to call the whole thing off?

Sam grasped Libby's shoulders in his hands. His electric-blue gaze caught and held hers, sending a deadly charge right to her heart. It was all she could do not to steal the kiss that had been on her mind all during breakfast and the interminable hours of fishing that followed.

"Having met your grandparents," Sam said, clearly oblivious to her inner turmoil, "I now understand why you have so much faith in forever afters. You, my dear, have been brainwashed."

"I have not!" Libby protested, all thoughts of kissing—and fishing—vanishing to parts unknown. She twisted free of his iron grip.

"Oh, yes, you have," Sam argued, shaking a finger at her. "And you'll never come face-to-face with reality as long as you hide up here at Wildwood, associating yourself with other romantics who share your belief in the myth. Talk about losing your perspective...."

"I am not hiding and I have not lost my perspective. For your information, Mr. Know-It-All, the reason I believe in happy marriages is because I'm the byproduct of a long line of them."

"Yeah, well, I'm not, and it's hard for me to relate—" He broke off, suddenly sneezing twice in succession, an action that surprised them both.

"Did you catch a cold Friday night?" Libby asked, frowning.

"I'm never sick," Sam said. He looked accusingly at Fetch, busily stalking an unsuspecting squirrel a few feet away. "I'll bet I'm allergic to that mutt of yours."

"I'll have you know that 'mutt' is my best friend," Libby snapped, ventilating her irritation at her stubborn boss. From the look of things, the longevity of her grandparents' marriage hadn't impressed him one whit. That left her only two more chances to show him the error of his ways.

"My point exactly," Sam countered coldly, adding, "You're living life secondhand up here, Libby. You have a dog for a best friend and nothing but a dream lover to keep you warm at night." He shook his head in disgust. "Your expectations are way too high. You're holding out for a hero who isn't going to show up."

"But he will," Libby protested, cut to the quick by his gloomy prediction.

"He *won't*. He doesn't exist." Sam sighed heavily. "Visit the real world sometime. Talk with some of its flesh-and-blood citizens. You might learn something."

"If it's going to make me as bitter as you, I think I'll pass," Libby exclaimed, hot tears of anger and frustration stinging her eyes. Mortified that she might break down in front of Sam, she whirled, managing two steps before he caught up with her and pulled her roughly into his arms.

He didn't say a word, just held her tightly to his thudding heart for a second. Then he tangled his hand in her hair, tugging on it until she had to look up at him. His fingertip captured the solitary tear snaking its way down Libby's cheek. He touched his tongue to it and then covered her lips in a long, hard kiss before he released her to step abruptly back. "Did you say lunch is at noon in the restaurant?"

Dazed, Libby managed a half nod.

"I'll be there."

A second later, she stood alone on the dock.

True to his word, Sam walked to the entrance of the restaurant at high noon. Fresh from a shower, his hair still slightly damp, he wore the last of his emergency clean clothes: pleated khaki pants and a rust-colored knit shirt. He restlessly paced the sidewalk while he waited for Libby, his thoughts ricocheting inside his head.

He'd never meant to hurt her this morning, wished he could take back everything he said. But he couldn't, and maybe that was just as well. Libby did exist in a dream world. It was high time for her to realize she was wasting the best years of her life waiting for some joker to come in and sweep her off her feet.

So what do you care? he asked himself sternly, abruptly halting his prowl. Why did it matter that Libby had set her goals so high? Because her romantic fantasies would only make the closing of Wildwood that much more difficult for him and traumatic for her? Or was there another reason altogether?

Did Libby's dreams upset him because deep inside he knew he wasn't the star of them and would never be able to offer what she wanted? Maybe, Sam decided. He didn't know for sure. He *did* know it was past time to escape Wildwood and the spell woven around it. His starry-eyed manager was fast wearing him down. And if he didn't watch his step, he would find his house that much more lonely when he returned to Memphis and he just might discover that a successful law practice wasn't a substitute for happiness after all.

"Hi. Been waiting long?" Libby's voice jerked him back to reality. Sam whirled toward the sound, his sweeping gaze missing not one detail of her voile dress, from the gathered skirt to the row of tiny buttons running neckline to hem. Icy blue in color, the garment was belted with a sash that set off to perfection her tiny waist.

Sam abandoned all thoughts of leaving. "Just got here."

"Good." Libby let her eyes linger on him a second longer, anxiously verifying what just might be a good mood. Relieved, she put her hand on the door, pulling it open before Sam could assist and stepping into the restaurant. She paused just inside, scanning the area for the next two "ghosts," newlyweds named Sally and Dennis, whom Libby had checked into Wildwood late Friday night. Married a grand total of thirty-six hours, they were young and optimistic—absolute necessities for Ghosts of Marriage Present.

She spotted them almost immediately, sitting in a booth to one side, heads together and obviously lost in love. *Perfect,* Libby thought, smiling to herself as she wound her way over to them, Sam in tow. She greeted the pair with a smile, introducing Sam before she motioned him onto the seat across the table from the young couple.

Libby turned to her boss, now sitting shoulder to shoulder with her. "These two hail from Little Rock. They got married Friday." She smiled. "Sally tells me they hocked Dennis's motorcycle so they could honeymoon here."

"Congratulations," Sam murmured somewhat dryly. "I hope it was worth it." Libby noted the way his eyes lingered on Sally, who didn't look a day over seventeen with her big blue eyes and riotous black hair. He then glanced over at Dennis, a redhead with freckles, who didn't look much older. Libby could tell Sam thought they were teenagers.

Sally laughed. "It sure is to me. I had a heart attack every time he got on that old thing. He won't need it anymore anyway. We just live a block from campus and I have a very reliable car."

"Dennis is a sophomore at the University of Arkansas," Libby interjected at that point, sensing Sam's unspoken questions.

"Really?" Sam said, and Libby felt some of the tension leave his body. "I graduated from there."

"No kidding?" Dennis said. "What was your major?"

"Law."

"I'm going to be an accountant," the redhead told him proudly.

Sam looked Sally's way. "Do you attend the university, too?"

"I went one semester," the young woman replied. "That's where I met Dennis. When we decided to get married, my parents told me I was on my own. So did his. I guess they were trying to discourage us. None of them think this marriage is such a good idea." She shrugged. "Anyway, I quit school and got a job so we could pay the bills and take care of his tuition and books. I work at the University's day-care from seven-thirty until four every day."

"In other words, you've thrown away your education to give Dennis one?" Sam said, rather sarcastically to Libby's ears. She looked anxiously toward her guests, hoping her boss hadn't offended them.

He hadn't. "It's just until I graduate," Dennis assured him, obviously undaunted. "Two-and-a-half, three years, tops. Then it'll be Sally's turn to go."

"You don't mind that your wife is sole supporter?" Sam asked.

"Oh, he has a job," Sally interjected. "Dennis works at the Easy Stop convenience store from three-thirty to midnight every night."

Sam's eyes widened in shock. "Let me get this straight. You work from seven-thirty to four. He works from three-thirty to midnight. Just when do you two plan on seeing each other?"

Dennis and Sally both laughed. "From midnight until seven-thirty, of course."

Sam was suddenly at a loss for words.

Dennis, who'd obviously picked up on Sam's stupefaction caught the lawyer's eye, winked and grinned. "We're probably going to lose a lot of sleep, huh?"

His new wife jabbed his ribs with her elbow and then turned to Sam. "It's really not as bad as it sounds. We do have the weekends free—when Dennis isn't at guard drill, that is."

"He's in the National Guard, *too*?" Sam couldn't believe his ears. Overwhelmed by the myriad obstacles these two foolish hopefuls faced, he could see no chance of survival for this marriage—none at all. Yet here they sat, all smiles and big plans for a lifetime together. How could they be so optimistic in the face of all their problems? he wondered.

At that moment Dennis dipped his head to steal a quick kiss from his lady, and the glow of love, multiplied by two, revealed the answer. Dennis and Sally didn't even know they had problems.

Sam functioned methodically through the luncheon that followed—yet another meal on the house. Lost in thought and oddly depressed, he said little, speaking only when directly addressed and eating his submarine sandwich without really tasting it. Two hours after he and Libby entered the restaurant, they left it, again via the kitchen.

By the time Sam walked Libby to her door, he'd sneezed several more times and his temples throbbed with a dizzying pain. Crediting the uncharacteristic headache to a rather stressful morning, he said a hasty goodbye and turned to go.

"What's your hurry?" Libby said, catching his sleeve in her hand.

"My head's hurting. I want to think. I thought I'd take a walk in the woods...alone."

Sufficiently rebuffed by that qualifier, Libby quickly released him. "All right, then. Would you like an aspirin before you go?"

"I've got some, thanks." Again he turned to leave.

"Sam?"

"Hmm?" He kept his back to her.

"Do you think they'll make it?"

Suddenly too tired to bandy words with her, Sam didn't pretend to misunderstand the question. He turned slowly back around. "Oddly enough, I do."

Libby sighed, walking to the log rail framing her porch. She plopped down on it and propped her elbows on her knees. "I'm not so sure, myself," she murmured, counting each reason off on her fingers as she proceeded to tell him why.

"They'll make it," Sam interjected firmly when she'd used up the last available digit.

Libby frowned over at him. "What makes you say that? The odds are against them, and you know it."

"The odds might be against them," he replied. "But they've got something more important *for* them."

"What's that?" she asked, tilting her head to one side.

"Love."

Libby smiled at him. "Love? Did you say *love*?"

Sam nodded.

"But I thought you said there was no such thing," she teased ever so softly.

"Maybe I've been wrong," Sam said. "About a lot."

Chapter Seven

Maybe, indeed, Libby silently agreed, watching Sam stride off in the direction of the old hiking trail. More than a little pleased by the apparent success of Wildwood's latest two ghosts, she leaned back against the log post that supported the porch roof. She closed her eyes, making the best of this precious moment alone to soak in the peace and quiet around her.

"Hey."

Libby's eyes flew back open to find Sam had returned and now stood inches away, his feet on the moss-covered ground, his arms crossed over the porch rail, inches from where she sat.

"Hey, what?" she answered softly, intensely aware of his tousled blond hair, so touchably close, and the frosty blue of his eyes.

"I was just wondering... How'd you ever talk those two into sharing part of their precious honeymoon with us?"

Libby grinned. "I bribed them," she admitted, impulsively adding "free accommodations on their first anniversary" in the hopes he might give a hint as to the current status of Wildwood's future.

"I should have known," Sam said, with a rueful shake of his head. "And just what are you going to do about them when I sell out tomorrow?"

Libby nearly fell off her perch, holding on to it, and her smile, with difficulty. "Something tells me they'd probably settle for a cash donation."

He laughed shortly then left her, headed determinedly down the road to the trail and the woods, several yards away. Her good mood now in the gutter, Libby gloomily watched his progress. *Maybe I should just forget this whole thing,* she mused. Clearly her boss had made up his mind, and every minute she wasted trying to make him change it could well prove perilous to her heart.

But what would she do with her time when he left? Libby tried to picture herself as she'd been pre-Sam—working all the time, daydreaming when she wasn't, satisfied to live and love vicariously while she waited for her own Mr. Right.... Her heart constricted. She knew she could never go back to that sort of existence, and realized with a start that the imminent closing of Wildwood didn't seem to be nearly as distressing to her as the possibility that she might never see its owner again. She leapt abruptly to her feet.

"Sam!"

He didn't stop this time, but pivoted to face her, continuing his walk with slower backward steps.

"You won't be long will you? We're scheduled to meet the Ghosts of Marriage Future, first set, in an hour."

Sam halted abruptly, his sagging shoulders and downturned mouth revealing his impatience with the whole thing.

"*First* set? For God's sake, Libby, how many sets are there?"

"Just two," she quickly assured him.

Nodding weary resignation, Sam turned and headed down the narrow trail into the dense woods.

Libby didn't tarry long on the porch, but made her way to the office to verify that her nephew had showed up for work at noon. Minutes later, she took a walk of her own—up to the pool, down by the lake and over to the little wedding chapel situated not far from it. The nondenominational structure, a graceful blend of stained glass and wood, had been the site of several intimate ceremonies since the renovation of Wildwood. Libby often escaped to the quiet there to think.

She walked slowly down the center aisle, absently trailing her hands over the carved oak pews on either side. Sunlight streamed through the collage of tinted glass behind the altar, casting a brilliant reflection on the hardwood floor. Libby walked deliberately through the colorful rays, watching the shades play over her dress and skin.

She held out her hand as though to capture the kaleidoscope, noting how her fingers turned first blue and then red—much like her moods of late. Smiling at her foolishness, she walked over to the piano near the front of the room, placed so the person who played it could see the wedding couple. She sat on the bench, her back to the rows of pews, and touched one of the keys, wincing at the note that emanated. The damp air from the lake wreaked havoc on the musical instrument. As a result, it had to be tuned before each wedding and was badly in need of it now.

Nonetheless, Libby played several of the pieces she'd learned as a youngster, humming accompaniment. When she'd performed every song in her meager repertoire, she glanced at her watch, noting she had another ten minutes left to kill before meeting Sam.

She laid an arm on the spinet and rested her forehead on it. Absently she touched the ivory keys, picking out a tune that she'd always loved—one that represented her lifelong hopes and dreams.

"Ahh, 'The Wedding March,'" a very familiar voice murmured from right behind. "Very appropriate."

Libby jumped as though she'd been shot. She jerked her hand back from the keys and, face flaming, looked over her shoulder at Sam. "What are you doing here?"

"I heard music. I came to investigate." He hooked his thumbs in his pants pockets and scanned the room, turning slowly to take in every last detail. "Do you have many weddings here?"

"We've had a few."

He nodded. "And were you in them?"

"Only as a witness," she replied, somewhat defensively since she didn't quite trust that icy gleam in his eye or the line of questioning. "When the couple needed one."

"I'll bet you found that damned frustrating."

She got to her feet, frowning at him. "What's that supposed to mean?"

He shrugged. "You're obviously hung up on weddings and honeymoons. And though you say you're single by choice, I expect it must be disappointing to never be in one of your own."

"I am not hung up on weddings!" Libby exploded, hurt by his sarcasm. She half wished he'd gotten lost in the woods. Obviously all that fresh air hadn't agreed with him.

"You could have fooled me," Sam retorted coolly.

"Well, you're wrong, and you're confusing waiting for the right man with being hung up on weddings."

"Does that mean if the right man came along you'd welcome him with open arms—wedding or no?"

"Yes. No. I mean—"

"Never mind," Sam said, cutting short her stammering reply. "I know the answer." He looked at his watch. "Why don't we just get on with this? Are our ghosts meeting us here?"

Baffled by his chameleon mood swing, she responded, "No. We're meeting them at their cabin, unit twelve."

"That big one at the edge of the woods, right?" Sam asked, explaining, "I walked by it just a minute ago."

She nodded briefly, brushing past him as she stalked up the aisle to the door. Sam stared after Libby, unrepentant, even though he knew he'd riled her again. He'd done it on purpose this time, in an attempt to find out if she might be willing to compromise her dreams and settle for a fling with a very lonely divorce lawyer who really wanted her but couldn't tolerate the thought of a more binding commitment.

She'd given him her answer—loud and clear. Put in his place once and for all, he intended to keep that answer firmly in mind for the rest of the weekend. He also intended to keep his distance . . . no more stolen kisses. They were lethal, especially in combination with the romantic atmosphere that had caused him all this misery in the first place. Disgruntled by that difficult decision, he exited the chapel to catch up with Libby, whose temper-fueled stride had carried her several yards down the road.

"How's your headache?" she demanded in a barely civil tone when he joined her. Sam noticed the angry set of her jaw and how she kept her eyes straight ahead. She moistened her lips with her tongue, a tantalizing action that challenged his recent resolutions not to kiss her again.

"Alive and well," he snapped, irritated at his weakness where she was concerned.

"Did you take anything for it?"

"No."

"Why not?" She slowed her steps and looked over at him.

"Because I don't want anything."

"That's stupid, I'll get you some aspirin."

"I don't take aspirin."

"Then I'll get you something else."

"I'm okay, dammit!"

Libby halted completely then, whirling to confront Sam. Her flushed face and blazing eyes surely mirrored his own. "There's no reason to shout at me," she said. "I'm only trying to help you."

"I'm not shouting," Sam shouted. He winced when he heard the echo of his voice, lowering it slightly to say, "And you're not helping me at all, woman. You're making me crazy."

"Well, you aren't doing my mental well-being any favours, either."

They glared at each other, both steaming, a scenario that reminded Sam of two bulls locking horns. Suddenly hit with the absurdity of their latest argument, he burst into laughter. Libby, however, failed to see the humor of the situation.

"Don't you dare laugh at me," she said.

"I'm not," he protested, still doing just that.

Libby threw her hands up, snorting her exasperation. "I think it would be better for all concerned if I just cancelled the next ghosts. I'll get you a rental car. You can go home tonight—"

"Oh, no, you don't," Sam interjected, now sobered. "I promised you my weekend, and you're going to get it."

"But I don't want it anymore," Libby argued.

"We made a contract. It stands," he told her, turning on his heel, striding off toward unit twelve, now mere feet away. Libby ran after him, catching up just as he stepped onto the porch and knocked on the door.

It opened immediately to reveal a tall, dark-haired man who looked very familiar to the lawyer. Sam stood silently, not quite able to place him.

"Hi, Pierce," Libby said, stepping up to take charge. "Hope we're not late."

"You're right on time," the man, who looked to be early forties, assured them with a friendly smile. "Come on in, Gina's out back on the deck, soaking up a little sun."

They made their way through the livingroom, which was quite similar to the others at Wildwood, with the exception of a skylight and a few extra square feet. Pierce opened a pair of French doors and stepped out onto the wooden deck in back, smiling at his honey-haired wife sitting on one of the lounge chairs. Libby quickly made introductions.

Gina nodded in greeting and moved as though to rise, halting when Libby exclaimed, "Don't get up."

"But I need to stretch," Gina replied, reaching out a hand. Her husband took it, helping her to her feet. As she straightened and stood, she tugged her oversized sweatshirt down over her midsection to mold what looked to Sam like a good ten-and-a-half months' worth of pregnancy. His eyes nearly popped out of his head.

Obviously seeing his alarm, Gina laughed. "Now don't panic," she said. "I'm only six months along. Twins."

"Pierce and Gina are from Memphis, too," Libby told Sam as she seated herself in one of the other chairs. She motioned for him to do the same.

"No kidding," Sam murmured, sitting and then turning to face Pierce, who'd seated himself near his wife's lounger. "That may explain why you look so familiar to me. Have we met before?"

"I was an expert witness on one of your cases several years ago," Pierce replied. "The old man suing the department store."

Sam nodded. "Oh, yes. I remember now. You're a doctor, aren't you?"

Pierce nodded.

Sam eyed Gina with a worried look. "Isn't it common for twins to be premature?"

"Yes, but I should be okay. I do have an M.D. in my pocket after all, and though orthopedics is his specialty, he'd do in a pinch." She winked at her husband. "We've been married seven years and have never missed an anniversary trip together. I couldn't let a little thing like twins stop me. Besides, this may be the one and only trip we will ever make without toting diapers, bottles, formula, et cetera, et cetera."

"These are your first, right?" Libby commented with a smile, though she well knew the answer.

"Yes," Pierce said. "We'd almost given up. We're very lucky."

"Do you want boys, girls or one of each?" Libby then asked.

"We want healthy babies and we want many more," Gina told her. She patted her protruding tummy. "These two are the embodiment of our hopes, our dreams, our future together." She turned to Sam. "Do you have any kids?"

"I'm not married," he replied.

"What about you?" Gina asked Libby.

"I'm not married, either," Libby told her. She slid a sidelong glance in Sam's direction, noting that his smile had vanished.

Pierce laughed softly. "What's an unmarried divorce attorney doing owning a honeymoon hotel?"

"That's exactly what I've been asking myself all weekend," Sam muttered, getting to his feet.

"Don't let him tease you," Gina said, walking back to her chair. She settled herself on it and glanced out toward the woods nearby. "You have such a lovely place here. I can't tell you how pleased we were to find out about it. We plan to come back next year."

"We'll be glad to have you if Wildwood is still here," Libby said. "Sam is thinking of selling out."

"But why?" Gina asked. "Judging from the number of guests, the resort is doing well."

Sam shrugged, not replying.

Pierce got to his feet, joining Sam at the rail where he stood. "Are you really going to sell?"

"Probably," Sam told him, much to Libby's dismay.

"I might be interested in buying. This looks like a good investment. Would you be willing to contact me first when you make a decision?"

"Why not?" Sam murmured.

Libby sank back in her chair, sick at heart though she should have been thrilled since Pierce would probably be willing to retain her, and maybe even her family, if he bought the place. That confirmed her earlier suspicion that it wasn't the fate of Wildwood keeping her up at night, but the owner of it. She didn't want Sam Knight to waltz out of her life as quickly as he'd waltzed into it. And that meant she'd done the unforgivable—fallen for a man she wouldn't marry.

What a god-awful mess.

Inordinately depressed by what she'd gone and done, Libby wanted only to flee to her cabin and hide under the bed until Monday. But escape was out of the question, of course. She and Sam had a contract and the Ghosts of Marriage Future, second set, awaited.

Libby and Sam didn't linger at unit twelve. Barely fifteen minutes later found the lawyer pocketing Pierce's business card as he descended the steps of the deck, Libby right beside him. When they rounded the corner of the cabin, out of earshot of the couple, she caught his arm, halting him.

Sam took one look at her, arched an eyebrow in surprise and held up his hands as though to ward off a punch.

"You're going to sell to him, aren't you?" Libby demanded, hands on her hips.

"Maybe," he replied. His eyes narrowed. "I should think you'd be pleased. I'm sure he'd keep the place as is, and he'd certainly keep you on."

Libby had no reply to that, knowing he spoke the truth. She should be happy, and if she weren't careful Sam was going to realize just why she wasn't. Quickly, she covered her near confession. "We don't know that for sure."

"True," Sam easily agreed, apparently satisfied with her reply. He glanced at his watch. "When and where do we meet the next crew of spooks?"

"Three o'clock at the pavilion by Lake Roosevelt," she told him. "We'll have to take the van." She turned then, leading the way back to the main parking lot, several yards away. Though openly curious, Sam asked no questions but whistled as he walked, a sound Libby found quite irritating. Clearly he was pleased with the idea of selling Wildwood to Pierce, and no wonder. It provided a guiltless way out for him.

In no time he would be back in his Memphis law office, doing his part to maintain the divorce rate. He would never give Wildwood or Libby Turner another thought. She, on the other hand, would be up to her neck in other people's happy endings—missing Sam and wondering if she'd blown her own.

Libby did the driving to the picnic area where the next ghosts—her entire family—had gathered to celebrate her grandparents' fiftieth anniversary. She and Sam said little on the trip over, both pretending to listen to the radio, both lost in thought. When she pulled into the parking lot, Sam stiffened in shock and gaped at the crowd milling about.

"My God," he muttered, eyeing the throng. "What is this?"

"A party for Mamaw and Papaw," Libby informed him, bringing the van to a halt. She killed the engine with a flick of the wrist and lay her arm over the back of the seat. "Besides my mother and brother, whom you've already met, you're going to make the acquaintance of my dad, my two younger sisters and various aunts and uncles, all of whom are happily married. You're also going to get to know their children, ranging in age from two weeks to thirty-five years."

Obviously a little awed by it all, Sam heaved a sigh. "Just what are you trying to prove here, Libby—that happy marriages do exist? Because if that's it, you're wasting your time. I've long since hollered uncle on that one."

Libby had to smile. "Have you now? Well, that is part of the reason, but only part. What you see over there is the future of every young married couple—kids, grandkids, great grandkids. Just think how much fun you're going to miss if you never get married—spend your whole life alone."

"Who needs a wife and kids? I do have family, after all."

"And how long has it been since you saw them?"

Sam rubbed his chin, clearly trying to remember. "Well, I ate lunch with my mom Easter Sunday. She's living in Cleveland now with my stepdad. As for my pop, well, he's remarried, too, and living in Hawaii. I haven't seen him in years."

"I figured as much," Libby said with a brisk nod. "And what about Ramona? How long since you visited with her—and I don't mean at the office."

"Umm . . . we went to dinner and a movie for her birthday."

"That was in June!" Libby scolded, shaking her head in disbelief. "You might as well be a hermit."

Sam squirmed under her censure. "All right. All right. Let's get on with this." He put a hand to his still-pounding temples. "I don't suppose you have any of that aspirin on you."

"As a matter of fact, I do," Libby told him, reaching into the glove box to retrieve a tin, which she handed to him. "Do you get these headaches often?"

"I never have headaches." He took two of the tablets, tossing them into the back of his throat and swallowing. Libby who couldn't swallow a pill without water if her life depended on it, watched in astonishment, choking for him. Sam then lifted the door handle and got out of the van. He waited at the front until Libby joined him. Together, they walked toward the noisy group clustered in and around the picnic pavilion.

Halfway there, Libby's older brother, Gil, joined them, greeting Sam with a nod and a smile. "Glad to see you. Papaw's been bragging on the fish he caught this morning, and since I've never seen a bass that weighed twelve pounds, I want an eyewitness report."

Sam laughed at the exaggeration, visibly relaxing, and proceeded to enlighten Gil on the details of their catch, the largest of which was big all right but nowhere near twelve pounds. Smiling, Libby eased away from the pair and made her way to her parents and grandmother, who sat at a picnic table under the shelter of the pavilion.

The breeze caught and disseminated the smell of hickory smoke, good food and rain. Libby looked skyward, noting with some regret that threatening storm clouds now covered a good three-fourths of the blue dome, blocking the sun and heralding the arrival of the weather that had threatened since Saturday morning. Libby knew she could expect a thundershower—or worse—before dawn. She grimaced at the thought of Sam driving through yet another storm.

Her mother, Elise, who'd managed to escape the kitchen for a while, smiled a greeting and motioned for Libby to join the three of them. Libby did, slipping past her petite mom to step over her dad's long legs. She then plopped down on the wooden seat between him and his mother with a weary sigh.

"I see you brought your boss," Elise commented, peeking around her husband, Jessie.

"Yeah," Libby muttered.

"Making any progress with him?" Jessie asked, draping his powerful arms over the shoulders of all three women. Libby, who'd given them a rather sketchy version of her problems over the phone the night before, shook her head and snuggled closer.

"He's still going to sell out, then?" her grandmother asked.

Libby nodded. "It looks that way, and after all our efforts to talk him out of it. God, but he's stubborn."

Her dad chuckled at that and tugged a lock of her hair. "What's that old saying? Takes one to know one?"

"I'm not stubborn," Libby protested. "I'm...dedicated, and to a very noble cause."

"Employment?" her mother questioned. She leaned forward so she could better see Libby, resting her elbow on her husband's leg.

"No, marriage," Libby replied, "Sam doesn't believe in it. That's why he wants to get rid of Wildwood. I've been trying to show him the error of his ways. I thought that might help him change his mind."

"What he needs is a good woman to turn him around," Martha said with a firm nod.

"Forget it," Libby responded gloomily. She thought of her own futile efforts to do just that and the price she'd paid. "He's a lost cause."

"Cheer up," her dad interjected, certainly misunderstanding the reason for her gloom. "Even if he sells, you might get to stay on, and if you don't, well, you're young and highly qualified to find another position."

"I suppose so," Libby answered, not about to admit that job security—especially her own—was the least of her worries at the moment. She glanced over at Sam, now deep in conversation with Gil and her two younger sisters, Joanne and Pennie, and their grandfather. The five of them were laughing. Sam looked totally at ease with the Turner bunch, and, just for a moment, Libby closed her eyes, letting her wildest fantasy to date run free.

She envisioned a wedding, a Wildwood wedding, with all her beloved family members present. She heard music, smelled flowers, saw herself, a vision in her flowing white gown, and Sam, so utterly handsome in . . . What? Armor? *Shining* armor? Her eyes flew open wide. Her gaze swept Sam. She took note of his twinkling eyes, his broad smile, his easy chuckle. He wore no armor and never would, but something deep inside Libby told her he just might be the one for whom she waited. *Wouldn't you know it,* she thought. *When my knight finally shows up, he doesn't believe in happily ever afters.*

At that moment Sam's eyes found hers. He noted how quickly she looked away and the guilty flush that stained her cheeks. What was going on? he wondered, tensing slightly. Was his manager plotting yet another specterly visit? Lord, but he hoped not. He'd encountered just about enough of them for one day and felt like hell to boot.

The man next to Libby said something to her then. She looked back Sam's way, smiled and raised a hand, crooking her forefinger to beckon to him. Murmuring a "See you later" to her bragging grandfather and doubtful siblings, Sam walked over.

Libby met him, slipping her arm through his to lead him to her mother, grandmother and a man Sam presumed must be her father. He was right.

"Sam, I'd like to introduce you to my dad," Libby said, proceeding to do just that.

"Welcome to our little get-together," Jessie said, standing to extend a hand. Sam found his eyes level with the huge redhead's mustache and gulped, remembering that morning's teasing comment about Libby's sweatshirt and her subsequent warning. She may have been joking, but she certainly hadn't exaggerated her father's size.

"Nice to be here," Sam murmured, taking that hand and trying not to wince under the powerful grip. He could only hope Libby's dad didn't read minds since a few broken fingers might be considered just punishment for the lustful thoughts Sam had harbored about the man's daughter that day.

"Are you enjoying your stay at Wildwood?" Elise Turner asked.

Sam opened his mouth to reply, jumping nervously when the unexpected clang of an old-time chow bell filled the air and bounced around inside his aching head.

"Sounds like dinner is being served," Libby commented. "Do you like barbecue?"

"Love it," Sam told her, trying to ignore his suddenly churning stomach.

"Then we'd better grab a plate and get in line," she responded. Nodding to her relatives, she took his hand leading him to the smoking grills. Two steps away from their destination, he halted abruptly, unable to tolerate one second longer the sight or smell of the spicy food.

"I'm really not very hungry," he murmured. "You go ahead and eat a bite. I'll take a walk down by the lake."

"But—" she protested, frowning.

"Go. Enjoy yourself." He broke away, pivoting to step out from under the pavilion.

Libby caught up with him before he got a yard away. "What's wrong, Sam?" She touched a cool hand to his forehead.

"Would you just knock off the Nancy Nurse routine?" he snapped. "There's nothing wrong with me. I'm just not hungry. Now go back and spend some time with your grandparents."

"Okay, okay," she retorted, whirling to leave him and his bad temper alone.

Sam watched her until she disappeared into the crowd and then made his way on down to the lake, about fifty yards from the picnic tables. He leaned back against a towering oak tree, bending his knee to prop one foot on it and breathing deeply of the cool air.

He glanced at the gathering storm clouds and then at his watch, verifying that it was early yet in spite of the dusky dark. He scanned the familiar lake, his thoughts on all the times he'd camped here, first as a Boy Scout and then later on his own. He recalled the cookouts, the fishing, the canoe races.

Sam's gaze shifted automatically to the nearby launch ramp and boat house. Lost in his memories, he idly watched two little girls crawling into one of the canoes tied to the dock, a canoe much like the one he'd owned briefly as a teenager. The craft had been a present from his dad, already divorced from Sam's mother and living in Missouri at the time. Sam remembered the look on his mom's face when the canoe had been delivered. Unable to afford such expensive presents on her meager salary, she'd been hurt and angry, perceiving the gift as a bribe to win Sam's loyalty.

He remembered an accusing phone call, shouts and tears. His mother returned the canoe to the store the next day and sent the money back to his father. That, of course, resulted in yet another phone call, more accusations, more tears....

Sam sighed, blocking the unpleasant memories from his mind as he had so many times before. What was the point in rehashing them now? Those miserable days were long gone and best forgotten. And his parents, who married only because Sam's mother was pregnant with him, had finally found mates with whom they were happy. Sam suddenly remembered Libby's comment that love, and not sex, was the key ingredient to a happy marriage. He thought of his parents' troubled union and of his own, both based on physical attraction. He acknowledged that Libby might just have a point. Maybe marriages based on true love—like the ones he had seen today—did have a better chance for success.

The sound of laughter drew Sam's eyes away from the children playing in the canoe. Looking toward the lighted pavilion, he saw Libby, plate in hand, and all those other Turners. He took note of their friendly faces, their smiles, their easy camaraderie. The place overflowed with love. His heart twisted. Suddenly he envied Libby her forever-after roots, wondered if it were too late to put down a few of his own.

A child's squeal of fright jolted Sam from his reverie. He whirled toward the sound, his anxious eyes scanning first the dock and then—when he didn't spy the children or their canoe—the inky lake. He spotted the bobbing craft immediately, now untied and several yards out into the water with its preschool passengers still aboard. Sam sprang to life, loping to the end of the dock. He reached it milliseconds after a young woman, who was obviously their mother. Nearly frantic, the petite blonde shifted the toddler she held onto her hip and shrieked a warning to the youngsters, ordering them to sit still until she got help.

They didn't, of course, instead scrambling to the side of the vessel nearest their parent, a move that tipped the canoe and sent them both tumbling into the water. Their screams of terror rang out, mingling with the hysterical cries of their mother.

Sam stepped out of his shoes, shoved his glasses at the woman and dove into the familiar waters.

Chapter Eight

Oblivious to the drama at the lake, Libby sat with both her sisters on the fringes of the activity in the noisy pavilion. She laughed at a colorful recounting of her youngest sister's latest escapade and glanced absently toward the oak tree where her boss stood. But he wasn't there anymore. Lazily, Libby scanned the shoreline, the wooden dock where a rather agitated-looking young woman with a baby stood and the nearby boat house. Still no Sam.

At that moment the woman's faint cry of fear reached Libby's ears. Libby tensed, straining to see what could be wrong. Instantly, she spotted the overturned canoe several yards from the dock. Leaping to her feet, Libby counted one—no, two—small children in the lake, one of whom had managed to grab on to the craft. The other youngster bobbed in the water several feet away from it.

Stomach knotting in fear, Libby shouted an alarm even as a solitary swimmer angled into her line of vision. He closed in on the pair with swift, sure strokes, and though

Libby couldn't possibly verify his identity at that distance, she knew instinctively who he was. She dropped her plate, racing toward the lake's edge. Other family members, now aware of the life-and-death struggle, followed, two of them taking to the water immediately.

Just as Sam reached the canoe, the child farthest from it disappeared from view. Without hesitation, the lawyer ducked beneath the surface of the lake. The seconds stretched. Libby exhaled her own pent-up breath in a sob of panic. She waded into the lake, ready to help, but halting abruptly when Sam resurfaced in an upward explosion of water, coughing…and alone. Terror for the drowning child rioted within Libby. She said a quick prayer as Sam sucked in a deep breath and once more submerged. Eternity passed before he burst from the lake again, gasping, choking and this time clutching priceless treasure.

Clearly the sputtering child was alive, and the lake echoed the joyful cries of Sam's reinforcements, just arriving on the scene. Cheers of the onlookers on shore filled the air, and Libby, standing knee deep in the water, impatiently swiped at the tears that blurred the happy scene.

Several confused minutes later, a very thankful young mother hugged her frightened children and then their savior. Amid a babble of congratulations to all of the rescuers, several of Libby's relatives coaxed the shaking woman and her saturated offspring to the shelter of the pavilion. Reassured, the crowd then dispersed in stages, gradually reassembling near the food.

When the last Turner had patted Sam on the back and wandered away, Libby hurled herself at him, throwing her arms around his midsection with an elation born of an emotional high. Clearly as exultant, he laughed and took a quick step forward, pushing Libby behind the cover of a towering oak, hugging her back with enthusiasm.

"You were wonderfu—" Libby began, words smothered when Sam dipped his head to capture her parted lips. He moved his mouth over hers, first tenderly, then with raw hunger. His tongue teased, invaded, leaving her weak and trembling in his arms. Lost in his kiss yet intensely aware of his lean, soaked frame, Libby slipped her hands into his back pockets to pull him even closer. Sam responded with a husky moan that danced up her spine and lodged in her heart. He slid his hands downward over the thin fabric of her dress, tracing the curve of her hips. His mouth trailed across her cheek to nibble her ear and nuzzle her neck.

"Ahem."

Libby and Sam sprang apart instantly, whirling to face Jessie Turner, now making his way to them over the rocky ground. The man's bright eyes swept them both, and Sam thanked his lucky stars for the tree that just might have concealed the position of his wandering hands . . . and hers. A guilty flush heated his body from head to toe.

If Jessie had seen, he graciously didn't reveal it, merely handing Sam a dry bath towel he'd conjured up from somewhere. "We've cut the wedding cake your mother made, Lib. You two want some?"

Libby looked at Sam, who quickly shook his head. He was in no fit state for bright lights and curious relatives. Besides he'd had enough of ghosts tonight, not to mention canoes, lakes and six-foot-four fathers.

"I think I'd better drive Sam back to Wildwood," Libby murmured, glancing down at her dress, as soaked from the body-to-body contact with her dripping boss as the wade in the lake. "We're both wet."

Jessie remained silent for a moment. His eyes searched Sam's face. Then he laid an arm across the younger man's shoulders. "That's one very happy mommy over there eating cake with her kiddos. You did a good thing."

"Thanks," Sam murmured uneasily, his face now flaming.

Jessie released him and looked Libby dead in the eye. "You take extraspecial care of our guest tonight, young lady. He looks in need of a little TLC."

Libby gulped audibly, obviously as flustered as Sam certainly was by her father's choice of words. "I, uh, will."

Jessie nodded. Then he squeezed Sam's shoulder, gave Libby a kiss on the nose and left.

An awkward silence followed his exit. Sam, thoroughly disgusted with himself for his inability to keep his distance from her—and in such a public place—dried his face and hair with the towel. He then thrust it at Libby, busy wringing out the hem of her full skirt.

She took it, swiping at her clothes in an effort that helped little. A second later, she handed the towel back to Sam. "Ready to go?"

"Almost," Sam muttered, taking the towel and doing a little clothes swiping of his own. That accomplished, he took one step in the direction of the parking lot only to halt with a groan when Friday night's wreck and tonight's grueling swim suddenly caught up with him. Every muscle in Sam's thirty-seven-year-old body revolted, leaving him exhausted, aching and weak as a kitten. On top of that, he felt another sneeze coming on.

"Are you okay?" Libby asked softly, slipping her arm through his to support him.

"Fine," he told her, nonetheless draping his arm heavily over her shoulders to continue his limp to the van.

Rain splashed onto the windshield just as Libby turned the vehicle into the drive of the resort some fifteen minutes later. She switched on the wipers so she could see the way to Sam's cabin, her mind on the last time the two of them had driven in a downpour together. She hadn't really known the man beside her then. Now she loved him. Tomorrow he would be gone for good. Libby sighed softly at the unfairness of life.

"Tired?" Sam suddenly asked from the seat beside hers.

"Sort of," she replied, not quite ready to admit the real cause for that wistful exhalation. She braked the van to a halt right at the edge of Sam's porch so he wouldn't get wet—as if that mattered at this point—and turned to him. "How about you?"

"Dead on my feet, and I've got water in my left ear."

She had to laugh at his disgusted expression. "Still got the headache?"

"That, too." He reached for the door handle, moving as though to open it, then hesitating. "You do remember that I'm leaving tomorrow and will need a ride to my car?"

How could I forget? she thought, aloud murmuring a simple, "I remember." Somehow she mustered a smile. "It's been a hell of a weekend, hasn't it?"

He laughed shortly. "To say the least."

The van was quiet except for the swish of the wipers and the beat of torrential rains against the roof. Sam's gaze found Libby's. He reached out, cupping her chin, running his thumb over her bottom lip before she captured that hand in both hers to plant a kiss in his palm.

Sam caught his breath and jerked his fingers free. "I've, uh, enjoyed every minute of my stay here, Libby, and that includes the visits with your ghosts. I just want you to know that they've shown me the error of my ways. I understand that romance is critical to love and that love is critical to a successful marriage. I'm not going to sell out. I'm not going to change Wildwood. You win."

Before a stunned Libby could respond to that unexpected mouthful, Sam stepped out of the van and into the rain. A heartbeat later he disappeared through the door of his cabin, closing it behind him.

"I won," Libby told the steering wheel, waiting for the exhilaration of triumph—the rush of a job well done. But her leaden spirit refused to soar, and victory was bittersweet. All she could think about was Sam's imminent departure.

How will I survive without him?

Mechanically, she put the van in motion and headed the short distance to her own cabin.

She was still wondering that at midnight. Wide-eyed and wide awake, Libby had verified the twelve o'clock shift change via telephone and now lay in her bed, knees bent to accommodate Fetch, sleeping stretched out at her feet. Gale-driven rain slashed against the windowpanes, adding fuel to the fire of her tempestuous thoughts.

Libby sat up suddenly, venting her misery on her feather pillows. Once they were fluffed to suit her, she plopped down again, tucking one under her head and hugging the other one tightly. She curled her body around the pillow, wishing she held not this inanimate bundle of ticking, thread and feathers, but the flesh and blood male in unit six. She was *that* far gone.

And where, exactly, *was* that? Nowhere, Libby gloomily decided, abruptly abandoning the pillows to crawl from the bed. She paced up and down the darkened room with agitated steps, her brother's cast-off football jersey billowing about her thighs with each pivot. Her thoughts were on Sam and how in the world she could stop him from exiting her life. Sure he would still be her boss if he didn't sell, but a long-distance one. And something told her that once he got back to his "real world" of divorce court, he would be lost to her.

What, oh, what, could she say or do to ensure a place in his life after Monday? Libby agonized as she marched. Surely there was something. Surely.

"Sex might do the trick," she mused aloud, halting in her tracks. Fetch raised his head at that, watching her with eyes that shone iridescently in the night.

"Now don't you say a word," Libby murmured defensively, glancing toward her pet. "I *am* over twenty-one, after all. That's certainly old enough to have an affair with the man I love."

But was that kind of relationship really the answer? Of course not, Libby decided a second later, marveling that after all these years of saving herself for Sir Right she would even consider such a thing. Hadn't she delivered a stinging lecture to Sam just yesterday on that very subject? Sex, no matter how exciting, wouldn't be enough to keep them together for long. Libby wanted longer than "long" from Sam Knight. She wanted forever.

Forever? From a man she'd known a little over forty-eight hours? Libby almost laughed at the crazy direction her thoughts had taken. Obviously Sam was right. She *had* gotten hung up on weddings and lost her perspective on reality. Well, she was about to get a grip on it again. Though her ghosts had done a fantastic job convincing Sam of the merits of romance, love and marriage, he was by no means ready to walk down the aisle. Especially with Libby, a woman he'd just met, might desire, but certainly didn't love.

"I guess I got a little carried away with this knight stuff, huh?" Libby said to Fetch as she sprawled across the bed. She sighed lustily. "So much for white steeds, castles and love at first sight. I barely know that man. What I feel for him must be physical attraction. Thank goodness he has no idea what I've been thinking. From now on it's strictly business between us, I'm keeping my distance."

Libby reached out to scratch behind her pet's ears, jumping nervously when lightning suddenly danced around the room. A split second later thunder rattled the walls. With a gasp of sheer fright, she buried her face in Fetch's back, covering her ears with her hands. That tactic did nothing to block out the next blinding flash or the blast of thunder immediately after it. Screeching her terror, Libby bolted for her jeans. So much for keeping her distance. Whether she loved Sam Knight or not, she needed him . . . right now.

"Libby! Let me in!"

Sam.

With a squeal of relief that she wouldn't have to brave the elements after all, Libby abandoned her mission and raced to the door. She opened it, throwing herself at Sam when he stepped inside. He welcomed her into his arms, then kicked the door shut and sidestepped Fetch, who'd leaped off the bed to welcome him. Together Sam and Libby stumbled to the couch, collapsing onto it.

"Are you okay?" Sam demanded worriedly, pulling her onto his lap. Heart thudding wildly against his rain-soaked undershirt, Libby never even acknowledged the question or raised her face from where she'd hid it against his neck.

"Hey," Sam said, grasping her shoulders to put an inch or two between their bodies. He cupped her chin with his fingers, raising her gaze to meet his. *"Are you okay?"*

"Now I am," she told him simply.

Sam relaxed and hugged her. "Thunder woke me up," he murmured in her ear as he began a soothing massage of her back. "I figured you might need some company, so I came on over."

"Thanks," she whispered, snuggling against him. Oblivious to the wet of Sam's clothes and skin, Libby shamelessly made the best of this last chance to cling to the man she probably loved, after all.

The clock chimed one before the lightning dimmed and the thunder died to a distant roll. Sam, now minus the undershirt, sat on the couch, his eyes on Libby who lay on her back beside him, her head on his thigh. The table lamp revealed that her own eyes were closed, and he wryly noted that while she'd relaxed noticeably in the past hour—maybe even to the point of actually getting some sleep—he'd done the opposite. His nerves were as taut as violin strings; his heart pumped double time.

And no wonder, he mused, letting his gaze caress Libby's threadbare football jersey just once more. The faded fabric hugged her full breasts and flat stomach. Its tattered hem, which had ridden up around her hips, revealed a tantalizing glimpse of lavender panties and every shapely inch of her smooth, bare legs. Sam swallowed convulsively, dragging his eyes away with difficulty even as he wondered what Libby would do if he gave in to his need to kiss and touch her awake.

Better not to know, he decided, clenching his hands into tight fists to keep them in line. She'd spent her whole life waiting for a man who could give her more than a one-night stand. He was leaving tomorrow.

So think of something else, he justly scolded himself, making an honest effort to do that. Deliberately Sam raised his eyes to inspect Libby's room, much like all the others at Wildwood, except for this and that touch that made it distinctly hers. He saw a ledger, calculator and pencils piled on the bedside table, items that attested to her secondary, practical nature. Inches away from those lay a dog-eared romance novel—the kind with a buxom heroine on the front and the happy ending inside—a testament to her dominant, not-so-practical nature.

Which side did he like best? Sam suddenly wondered again. The businesswoman? The dreamer? Or the intriguing combination of both? He still wasn't sure. He was sure he would miss her when he finally got into his car and headed home. Somehow in the past two days she'd become a part of his life. He couldn't imagine a moment without her cheerful optimism and sunny smile. Memphis was going to be damned dull.

"Sam? You asleep?"

He looked down to find her peering up at him with sleepy brown eyes. He grinned ruefully at her softly uttered question. Asleep? With a long-legged brunette in reach? Fat chance. "No."

Libby sat up then, putting her arm through his, settling her cheek on his biceps.

"That's another life you've saved tonight," she murmured. "And you were the one supposed to get the TLC."

"It's never too late," Sam replied with hopeful huskiness in spite of his recent resolutions to behave himself.

Libby smiled softly and shifted her position to face him, tucking her legs under her hips. She reached up to take hold of his glasses, gently removing them. She put them on the end table. "Can you see me all right?"

"You're blurry around the edges," he admitted.

"How blurry?"

"Very blurry," he qualified with a little laugh.

"But you can tell who you're with?"

"I *know* who I'm with."

"Good. And your other senses are all in excellent working order?" she persisted.

Clearly bemused by her questions, Sam nodded. "They are."

"What about your sense of touch?"

He grinned. "Especially that one."

"So you can feel this?" she asked, brushing her fingertips over his mouth, cheek and chin.

He sucked in his breath. "Yes."

"And this?" Libby slid her hand down over his neck and collarbone. She tangled her fingers in the golden-blond hair sprinkled there, before skimming downward over his ribs.

Sam wheezed his appreciation of her exploration. "Oh, yes."

"And this?" She traced the indentation of his navel.

Sam gasped and grabbed her brazen hand in his. "Any lower, and I'm not responsible for the consequences."

She laughed at him, but changed her strategy, leaning down to boldly press her lips first to the flesh over his pounding heart and then to the taut brown nipples on either side. He shuddered in response.

"Are you cold?" she asked, sitting back on her heels, frowning.

Sam winced at her foolish question and glanced down at his sweats, still a little damp from the rain and steaming from the overheat of his lower body. "A little damp maybe, but definitely not cold."

She sighed softly and shook her head. "Poor baby. You've been waterlogged ever since you got here. I sure hope you don't get sick."

"I'm never sick," Sam assured her, adding, "and you're probably as wet as I am." He reached out to test his theory, fingering the jersey, which *was* slightly moist from the contact with him. He grinned mischievously. "I sure like this nightie. Where'd you get it?"

Nightie? Libby had to look down to see what she had on.

With a gasp of disgust, she sprang from the couch. Sam grabbed her before she could get away, however, and laughing at her belated modesty, pulled her onto his lap.

He lowered his face to hers, stealing her token protest with his mouth. She shocked him with her eager response, pressing her curves to the hard wall of his body as the kiss exploded into an urgent mating of lips and tongues that set fire to a need he could no longer deny. Distracting her with his heated kisses, Sam eased Libby back onto the cushions, shifting his own position until she lay between him and the back of the couch.

Then he continued the sensual onslaught, trailing kisses on her neck, her chin, her cheek. His hands fanned the flames of mutual desire, touching, squeezing. He raised his head and smiled softly at her. "You forgot one of my senses."

Dazed, she frowned. "What . . . ? Oh. Which one?"

"Taste."

"Mmm. How *is* that one?"

"Let's find out." Sam caught the hem of the jersey, tugging upward until her breasts were bared to his hungry eyes and mouth. He tasted each, teasing the rosy tips to pebble hardness with his tongue. Libby gasped with delight.

"W-well?" she stammered breathlessly when he finally raised his head again long seconds later and smiled down at her.

"I'm not sure. I may need more time before I make a decision."

"Take as long as you like," she urged in a whisper. "Take all night."

Or the rest of our lives? he suddenly wondered, his narrowed gaze sweeping her flushed face. Libby's mahogany eyes glowed with passion and something more...something deeper... something very like love for him.

Sam tensed in her arms, at once sure that if he stayed with her one second longer, tomorrow would find their lives hopelessly tangled. He wouldn't know until too late if their magic moments together were anything more than the result of a weekend in a lovers' paradise.

"What's the matter?" Libby asked softly, obviously picking up on his dilemma. She framed his face in her hands.

"I just figured out what's wrong with this scenario," Sam replied.

"Oh?"

"That stupid mongrel of yours is sleeping on the job."

Libby laughed, raising up on one elbow to peer over Sam's shoulder at Fetch, sacked out on the bed. "So he is." She lay back down, hugging Sam. "I won't tell Dad if you won't."

"There's nothing to tell," Sam said, somehow finding the strength to ease out of her embrace. He stood up. "And won't be. I'm leaving."

"Leaving?" She sat up, pulling down her jersey, gaping at him. "You're *leaving*?"

He nodded firmly and headed for the door, bending down to scoop up the undershirt wadded on the floor as he passed it. When he straightened, the room tilted, Sam gulped and hastily groped for his glasses, attributing his dizziness to his vision.

"But why?" she asked.

"I'm not ready for this, Libby," he told her, pushing the glasses onto his face.

Her bright eyes swept his love-tensed body from head to toe. "You've got to be kidding."

"Mentally," he quickly qualified, flushing under her blood-warming appraisal.

Her face fell. "I . . . see."

Knowing he'd hurt her—exactly what he'd hoped to avoid—Sam stepped back to the couch. He sat next to Libby, taking her hand in his. "I want you. God. I want you. And maybe you want me...tonight. But what about tomorrow? I'm still leaving, you know. I have a job, a house, clients, responsibilities..."

So do I, Libby thought, heart sinking, *and I'd throw them all away for a lifetime of loving you.* But she said nothing. She heard the farewell in his voice. She finally knew the truth. He wanted her, but he didn't love her. And though it hurt that he didn't care as she did, Libby was ready to take whatever he *would* give.

"Don't look so sad," she told him, reaching out to touch his frown. "I'll settle for tonight."

"But I won't," he said, much to her surprise. "I've learned my lessons much too well. This weekend I've seen how happy two people can be. I won't settle for less. I want it all."

Libby was speechless with shock.

He smiled ruefully at her and twisted the garment he held. "Can't believe your ears? Well, I can't believe my mouth. And that tells me it's time to get away from here so I can think clearly. I've got to sort out my feelings."

"And then you'll come back?" she asked hopefully, finally finding her tongue.

"I don't know, honey. I just don't know. And that's why I can't stay here tonight. It wouldn't be fair to you."

Libby sagged back against the couch, sighing her frustration as she acknowledged the trouble with loving a knight. They were too damned noble. The fact that this particular one was probably also right didn't help her blue mood one bit. Clearly he was as confused as she was about their relationship. Clearly his mind was made up about leaving. She wouldn't shame herself by begging. It was time to give in gracefully.

"Hey, it's all right," she lied, somehow mustering a smile. "I understand."

Libby got to her feet, walking to the door and opening it to hurry him on his way. Hot tears stung her eyelids, ready to spill forth. She swallowed the lump in her throat.

Obviously relieved, Sam joined her there.

"I'll be very busy tomorrow," Libby told him as he stepped out onto the porch. "It might be better if Dad or Gil gives you a ride into town."

"Fine," Sam quickly answered with obvious relief. He turned to face her, standing in awkward silence on the shadowed porch. His eyes wouldn't meet Libby's. She knew he saw right through her flimsy excuse.

The air was pungent with the smells of lightly sprinkling rain. Water dripped from the trees, plopping onto the fresh blanket of leaves the chilly winds had strewn. Harmless now, lightning illuminated the distant sky, accompanied by the low rumble of thunder—sights and sounds of an Arkansas autumn night. Sights and sounds Libby usually cherished. But not *this* night . . . maybe not ever again.

Sam was leaving and with him, her peace of mind . . . and heart. Wildwood would never be the same.

"Good night," he said softly.

"Goodbye," she replied with remarkable calm, stepping back to close the door on her hopes and dreams.

Tears welled up in her eyes. Blinking them back impatiently, Libby managed one stumbling step away from it before she heard a tremendous crash outside. She whirled, lunging for the knob, and throwing the door open wide to find Sam lying on his back on the sodden ground at the bottom of the porch steps, motionless.

Terror gripping her heart, Libby ran to him.

Chapter Nine

Oh, my God," she cried as she squatted down beside Sam. She didn't know what to do, where to touch him first. He lay so still, looked so...dead. Her stomach knotted with anguish. She reached out a hand, tentatively, then pulled it back. "Sam?" No sound left her lips. She swallowed hard and tried again, louder. "Sam?"

He stirred slightly, groaned and opened his eyes, blinking against the sprinkling rain.

Relief washed over Libby, relief so immense she sagged with the weight of it. She dropped to her hands and knees in the mud, sucking air into lungs that labored around a hammering heart. "Are you okay? Is anything broken? What happened?" she finally gasped, swaying forward to block the rain from his face with her body.

He didn't answer, clearly breathless himself.

"Sam, say something," she demanded impatiently, grasping his shoulders, giving them a little squeeze. "Please."

"Wind . . . knocked . . . out of . . . me," he panted.

Libby put her flattened palm on his chest, gently rubbing the dampened flesh. "Take it easy," she coached. "Relax."

He did, in seconds managing to draw in enough oxygen for a gusty exhalation.

"Better?" she asked, now in control of her own ragged breathing and her near panic.

He nodded.

"What happened?"

"I don't know. One minute I was just fine, standing on the porch. Then it whirled and threw me off."

"You fell off the porch?" she exclaimed aghast.

"Yes."

"Oh, my God. Are you hurt? Can you feel your toes?"

"My toes are fine," he assured her, trying to sit up.

Libby wouldn't let him, planting both her hands firmly on his chest to hold him immobile. "Stay put. What about your legs? Can you move them?"

"They're fine, too," he said, raising one and bending his knee to prove it. Again he tried to sit up.

Again, she stopped him. "How's your back?"

"In one piece," he snapped, clearly out of patience. "And smack dab in a mud puddle. Will you let me up, for Pete's sake?"

She released him only momentarily, shifting her hands to his arm and then clutching tightly as he struggled to sit. Halfway up, he faltered and cursed. A second later found him flat on his back again, groaning.

"What's wrong?" Libby demanded, panic once again welling inside her. "What is it?"

"Dizzy. I'm so damned dizzy."

"You must have hit your head when you fell," she exclaimed, once more hovering over him. "You probably have a concussion or something."

"But I landed on my butt," he argued. He closed his eyes, swallowing hard. "Do you see my glasses anywhere?"

She scanned the area and found them in a nearby holly bush. After swiping at them with her none-too-dry football jersey, Libby pushed them onto his face.

"Thanks. Now go get some help. . . anyone."

"I'll get my cousin, Jim. He's in the office," Libby told him, scrambling to her feet and heading that direction. She made it halfway up her porch steps before she got a better idea and spun around.

Libby hurried back to Sam, kneeling beside him once more. "Why don't I call Pierce instead? He'll know what to do."

Sam nodded his agreement with that plan. Then, before Libby could move a muscle to carry it out, he caught her by the shirt tail. "Get some jeans on."

"Right," she agreed, a second later dashing up the stairs to her apartment to do just that.

"How do you feel?" Pierce asked Sam not ten minutes later.

The lawyer opened his eyes, downright pleased help had finally arrived. Chilled to the bone in spite of the blanket Libby had brought him, Sam was more than ready to get out of this perpetual rain and into a hot Jacuzzi.

"Don't ask," he murmured.

Pierce grinned down at him. Then he set to work immediately, feeling for broken bones. "Everything seems to be intact. Can you walk?"

"Hell, doc, I can't even sit up." Sam answered.

"He tried to just a second ago," Libby interjected from her spot near Sam's knees. "Made him dizzy."

"Exactly how far did he fall?" Pierce asked her, frowning.

"From the porch," Libby told him.

Pierce winced. "Did he hit his head?"

"He said he didn't."

"Hmm. Has he had a headache—been sneezing, dizzy sick to his stomach the past few days?"

"All of the above!" Libby exclaimed. "I don't think he's felt well all weekend."

Sam snorted his impatience. "Will you two just cool it with the third-person routine?"

"Sounds like an inner ear problem to me," Pierce said, clearly unperturbed by his patient's bad humor. "Think the two of us can get him inside?"

"No," Sam replied before Libby could.

She glared him into silence and turned to Pierce. "Probably not, if he's really lost his equilibrium. I could get my cousin, though. He's about Sam's size and works the desk weekends."

"Better do it then. I can't check Sam out here, and this rain isn't doing any of us any favors."

Libby did as requested, returning in minutes with Jim. Many grunts, groans and colorful curses later, the two men finally managed to get all of Sam's two-hundred plus pounds up the steps, in the house and deposited on the bed Libby had protected with an old sheet.

After thanking Jim and sending him back to the desk, Libby lingered by the bed, watching anxiously while Pierce took Sam's vital signs. By the time he finished his examination, Sam's face matched the white sheet on which he lay sprawled.

"It's your ear, all right," Pierce told him. "Left one. Middle and inner—probably the result of a cold or maybe allergies."

"But I'm never sick," Sam protested.

"You are now, buster," Libby said. She frowned thoughtfully at the doctor. "He got water in that ear earlier tonight. Would that have anything to do with it?"

"Probably didn't do him any good, but he's had this infection for days from the look of things." Pierce put all his instruments into the bag and zipped it. "Is there a pharmacy around here?"

"The nearest one's twenty miles away," Libby replied, adding, "and it won't be open until eight, though I suppose I could roust the owner from his bed if we need to."

"We don't," Pierce replied. "I have enough motion-sickness medicine to get him by for now. Then early Monday he'll need to get started on an antibiotic, as well."

"Just leave the prescriptions with me," Sam said. "I'll get them filled when I get home tomorrow."

"Home?" Pierce asked. "As in Tennessee?"

"Yes," Sam answered. "My car's supposed to be ready in the morning, and I should be back in Memphis by noon or shortly after."

"Who's driving you?" Pierce asked, frowning.

"No one," Sam told him.

The doctor laughed shortly. "Then you're not going anywhere. An infection like this will take two days, maybe even three, to clear up. Why, you'll be flat on your back until Wednesday, earliest, and I don't want you driving until Friday."

"But I've got appointments, clients, court—" Sam began.

"Cancel them," Pierce said firmly. He extracted a small bottle of tablets from his bag, tipping six into Libby's palm.

"Two every four hours with food. Should help the nausea and the dizziness—may even knock him out. At any rate, he won't be able to walk alone for a day or two, so keep an eye on him. He's liable to fall and hurt himself if he tries to get up."

"He can stay here," Libby promised with mixed emotions. Relieved that Sam had no broken bones and a treatable illness, she relished the idea of having him around another day or two.

No matter what it cost her in peace of mind and heart.

Pierce promised to look in on Sam before he and his wife checked out the next day. He refused any pay, cheerfully suggesting that Libby deduct his fee from his bill. Smiling her thanks, she agreed. The minute the door closed behind him, she turned to Sam, who lay glowering his disgust with it all.

"I'm not staying here," he told her.

"You have to," Libby retorted. "Doctor's orders."

"But where will you sleep?"

"The couch. It's quite comfortable and plenty wide."

"So it is," he murmured, flushing. Their gazes locked for just a moment as both remembered just how comfortable and wide it really was. Then Sam glanced away, clearing his throat rather nervously to Libby's discerning ears.

In an effort to avoid a painful walk down memory lane, she deliberately turned her thoughts to the problems at hand. Libby walked over to the bed and stood, hands on hips, looking down at Sam. Her eyes swept his body, most of which was wet or mud splattered. She wrinkled her nose with exaggerated distaste.

"You need a bath, not to mention clean clothes."

"*You're* telling *me*?" he grumbled, oh-so-carefully raising his head just enough to rearrange the pillow under it.

"And since you can't get to the bathroom," she continued, as though he hadn't spoken, "that means a sponge bath." She pivoted sharply, heading to the kitchen for a pan of warm water.

His scowl had vanished by the time she returned with that, plus soap, a washcloth and a towel. A hopeful smile lit his face. "You're going to give it to me?"

"Don't you just wish?" she caustically replied, unceremoniously dumping her load on the bed. "Have at it, Mr. Knight. I'm going to get your things."

"But I'm sick," he protested dramatically. "I can't do this by myself."

"Get Fetch to help you," Libby said, motioning her pet to Sam's side and making tracks to the door. "He's got a mean tongue."

As she stepped out onto the porch, she heard Sam blurt, "Stupid dog!"

The cool, moist air felt wonderfully refreshing, blowing at the confusion in Libby's mind. How she loved that man. Was this a second chance to win him? she wondered. More time to prove to him that the romantic surroundings of Wildwood had nothing to do with the magic—the rightness—of their time together?

Maybe, she decided. But first she would have to prove it to *herself*. She'd been waiting for her knight a very long time, possibly using him as an excuse not to risk her heart. Sam wasn't the sort of man she'd expected. Yet she loved him. That meant she needed to take a serious look at her life and her dreams. Could it be Sam was right—that she was holding out for a hero who wasn't going to show up?

Maybe, again. She was, after all, no lady-in-waiting, but a very ordinary female. Wouldn't an ordinary male really be all she could ever hope for? Of course. And an *extra* ordi-

nary man like Sam Knight was a fantasy come true for any
woman.

Now all she needed to do was convince him of that, and
thanks to some crazy twist of fate she had several more days
to do it.

"I don't want anything to eat," Sam snapped. Propped
to semisitting on two pillows, he lay on Libby's bed, watching her every move. Next to him lay the "stupid" dog, his
great black head propped on Sam's denim-clad thigh, in
easy reach of the masculine hand absently petting him.

"But you have to eat," Libby argued, placing a bowl on
Sam's chest, which was now clean and encased in a dry T-
shirt. "You can't take this medicine without food."

"I'll get a bite later."

"You'll get a bite *now*." she told him, thoroughly exas-
perated. The past hour hadn't been much fun, thanks to
Sam's resistance to her help and his constant complaining.
Libby was past ready to dump him and his bad temper right
off the porch again. But what would that accomplish? she
asked herself. Clearly he hadn't lied when he said he was
never sick. He wasn't handling the new experience with
much grace.

Abruptly changing her tack, she softened her tone of
voice a little. "Look, it's after two o'clock, I have work to
do tomorrow. I need some sleep and I won't be able to get
it until you swallow these tablets."

"Oh, all right," he muttered, picking up the spoon and
taking a mini sip of canned chicken soup.

"Sa-am!"

"I'm eating it. I'm eating it!" he said tartly, lifting the
entire bowl to his lips and slurping with exaggerated enthusiasm. Libby turned on her heel, stalking to the kitchen for

his drink. The minute she turned her back, Sam placed the bowl on the floor for Fetch, who inhaled its contents.

When Libby returned with a glass of iced tea a minute later, Sam handed her the empty bowl.

Her jaw dropped. Her eyes narrowed in suspicion. "You've already eaten it?"

"Yes, ma'am," he replied with a guileless smile.

"Then take your tablets and drink this," she said, thrusting both at him.

He did, grateful for the cool liquid to settle his churning stomach. His temples throbbed with pain, as did his tailbone; his head swam every time he moved it. All he wanted was the same sleep Libby wanted.

"Thanks," she said when he handed her back the tumbler. "Now get some rest. You look like something Fetch dragged in."

"That's just about how I feel, too," he admitted, rubbing his weary eyes. She stole one of his pillows, which she tossed to the couch, and then fluffed the other one before reaching for the bedside light.

"Goodnight, Sam," she said softly when she'd turned it off.

Light from the nearby kitchen spilled out into the darkened bedroom, casting deep shadows that masked Libby's expression, but not the warm glow in her eyes. Sam's heart constricted. Suddenly he wanted to take her in his arms—show her how much she'd come to mean to him, tell her exactly how he felt about her now, this minute. But he couldn't, of course—not until absolutely sure that what he felt might last forever.

As she turned to leave him, Sam reached out, capturing her hand, pulling on it until she perched on the edge of the mattress. He awkwardly tugged a strand of her hair, loose and curling over her shoulder. "I guess I'm every nurse's nightmare, huh?"

"That just about sums it up," she told him, but she smiled.

"Thanks for your help, Libby. If it weren't for you, I'd still be laying out there in the rain."

"If it weren't for me, you'd be home, safe, in your own bed," she qualified, moving as though to stand.

Once again, Sam stopped her. "I could use a hug."

"You've got it," she replied without hesitation, leaning down to lay her head on his heart. He wrapped his arms over her back, holding her securely. She raised her face, kissing his chin and then his lips with a gentleness that made his blood boil before she eased out of his embrace.

"I'll turn the bathroom light on."

"All right."

"Night, Sam."

"Goodnight," he murmured regretfully, just as yet another kind of ache began—this one in his heart.

Libby heard the clock tick the minutes off one by one until it chimed at three. Then exhaustion caught up with her and she slept the sleep of the dead until ...

An anguished cry split the stillness of the night, yanking Libby to consciousness. She leapt to her feet in the semi-dark, disoriented, her heart hammering wildly, and stood in the middle of the room for a second trying to figure out what had wakened her.

Another cry, this one unintelligible, emanated from the vicinity of her bed, followed by a moan of sheer agony that made her skin crawl. Wide awake now, Libby flew across the room.

"What is it? What's wrong?" she demanded, reaching for Sam, who pushed her away and struggled ineffectually to rise. Beads of moisture covered his flushed face; his sweat-drenched shirt clung to his body. *He's delirious with fever* Libby thought. Her whole body tensed with anxiety. She put a hand to his forehead, which felt clammy cool to the touch. Not fever, she realized, but a nightmare.

He knocked her hand away. "Oh, God. Libby!"

"Sam," she cried, clutching his shoulders, trying to capture his flailing arms. "Sam!"

Caught up in his private hell, he twisted away, groaning, trembling.

"Wake up," she urged, falling over him to pin his hands between her upper body and his chest. She then framed his face with her own hands. "Please wake up. Please."

He ceased his struggles abruptly, opening his eyes to stare blankly up at her. The sound of his ragged breathing filled the room.

"It's me. It's Libby," she told him, brushing his damp-ened hair back off his face. "We're here in my apartment. We're okay."

He stared at her, unseeing, for what seemed an eternity before he wrenched his arms free. With a cry of relief, he threw them around her in a bone-crushing embrace even as he planted wild, hot kisses over her face and neck.

Libby tensed at the sudden onslaught and then collapsed on him, not resisting when he rolled over, taking her with him. Sam's mouth took hers again and again with a frenzy born of fear. She wrapped her arms around his waist, shifting to accommodate his weight, soothing him with touches and kisses every bit as urgent.

"I love you, Libby," he whispered huskily. "I love you."

He loves me. Heart singing, she sobbed her joy at those precious, precious words—words she'd waited a lifetime to hear. "I love you, too."

"I love you," he said again, as though he hadn't heard her reply. "Don't ever leave me."

"Never," she said, glorying in that promise. "Never."

That seemed to satisfy him. He relaxed in stages, until he lay full on top of her. Drooping his head down, he kissed Libby again, hard, and then rolled off her to lie gasping on the bed.

"Are you okay?" she asked, turning on her side to better see him.

He didn't answer for a moment, just lying there, staring at the ceiling as he drew in deep, shaky breaths.

"Sam?" She placed a hand on his heart, which still raced alarmingly.

He covered her hand with his, holding it secure. Libby felt his heart rate gradually slow—knew the moment he downshifted toward normalcy.

"Are you okay?" she asked again, propping her elbow on the bed and her head in her hand.

"I'm okay," he told her, half turning her way. He slipped his free arm under her neck. She rested her head on his shoulder, snuggling against him, relishing the nearness.

"Was it a bad dream?"

"A nightmare," he replied shortly, shuddering as vivid memories of what had to be a drug-induced phantasmagoria once more filled his head.

"Tell me."

"No, I don't want to talk about it."

"It might help," she urged. "Tell me."

He hesitated, then seeing the wisdom of her suggestion, haltingly began. "We were fishing."

"We who?" Libby asked.

"You and me...at the lake. We were in that old boat your granddad and I used Sunday." Sam took a deep breath. "It started to rain—"

"That's not surprising," Libby interjected.

Recognizing her attempt to lighten the mood, he managed a half smile. "The wind came up, and the waves. It was dark." He shook his head, not quite ready to relive the terror. "To make a long story short—"

"Don't," she said.

"Don't what?" he asked.

"Make a long story short. I want to hear it all."

He gave her a wry smile. Then he complied, telling her about the violent storm that had caused the lake to white cap, their boat to overturn.

"You were drowning, and I couldn't get to you. I swam in slow motion, fighting the water. You went under right before I reached you and never came up...."

His voice cracked. His heart began to thump erratically again. Libby, who obviously felt the change with her hand, raised her head to give him a quick kiss on the lips. "Shhhh, now. I'm right here ... in the flesh ... alive and well."

"Thank God," he murmured, squeezing her tightly. He swallowed convulsively. "What a dream. So damn real. Must have been the medicine...or maybe something I ate."

"Come on. The soup wasn't *that* bad," Libby gently teased.

Sam flushed guiltily, remembering he hadn't even eaten said soup, a very good reason that the medicine might have affected him so strongly.

"Know what I think?" Libby whispered, curving her body into his.

"Tell me," he replied, so grateful for her warmth. He placed a kiss on her forehead and her temple.

"Well, I read somewhere that dreams are our psyche's way of dealing with incidents we've tried to ignore. Maybe that accident this evening at the lake scared you more than you realized. I know it scared me."

"Maybe," he agreed thoughtfully. He closed his eyes. "Lord, I'm tired."

Libby sat up. "Then I'll let you sleep."

His eyes flew open wide. "Don't leave me," he blurted, clutching at her.

She hesitated, then lay back down beside him. "All right, if you'll promise to get some sleep."

"Nothing could keep me awake tonight," he assured her with a yawn. He settled himself more comfortably in the bed, wrapped both arms around Libby and closed his eyes. Gradually, languid warmth stole over him. He sighed softly and eased over the edge of slumber.

Oddly restless and unable to doze, Libby stared at the ceiling, the papered walls, the bookcase next to the window. She lay as still as possible, unwilling to share her insomnia with the man next to her. She looked longingly toward the kitchen, thinking of the late-night cola she'd missed earlier. She vowed to get it as soon as she could get out of the bed without waking him.

As Sam slipped ever farther into sleep, his breathing deepened. He relaxed his hold of Libby enough that she considered escape. Ever-so-gently, she raised the leaden arm flung across her waist, intending to roll over and sit up. Midmove, however, Sam foiled her plan by suddenly tightening his embrace, pulling her roughly back against the wall of his body.

Wide-eyed with surprise, Libby turned over to look at him, fully prepared to explain her mission. But his eyes remained closed, his breathing just as steady. He slept, and even in sleep wanted her near. What more could any woman ever hope for? she wondered, blinking back tears.

Lost in love for him, Libby abandoned the cola and hugged Sam back. Over and over she replayed his vow in her head, cherishing each precious syllable. He loved her . . . an unbelievable gift she didn't deserve, but gladly accepted. He wouldn't be leaving for several days, and then not for good. Her dreams had come true. Their life together would be wonderful.

Everything was going to be all right.

Sam blinked against the bright sunlight streaming onto his face. Sunlight? At Wildwood? Unthinkable, he decided, smiling to himself.

Gauging from the amount of light outside, Sam guessed the time to be sevenish. He realized the effects of his only dose of medicine should be worn off and raised just his head, moving it a scant inch from side to side to test for dizziness. The bed rocked gently, a sensation much like that of being in a boat.

Boat... boat...? What did he need to remember about a boat? Sam wondered, dropping his head back as he tried to focus the blurred images that flickered just beyond the screen of conscious thought. He felt a vague unease he couldn't explain. Impatiently shaking it off, Sam verified that he felt somewhat better in spite of the persistent vertigo—much better, in fact—and hungry as a grizzly.

He raised his arm in a lazy stretch, a move that alerted him to the position of his body, wedged tightly between something huge and furry, which turned out to be Fetch, and some *one* slender and soft... Libby. Sam patted the dog's head and then turned his back on him, since oversize mutts were not his idea of acceptable sleeping partners.

Sleeping partners? Libby? Sam frowned even as he edged closer to her, trying to remember just why she might be in his bed. The last thing he recalled was a tender good-night and his intense longing to spill his guts to her. Surely he hadn't...? But of course not. He knew he had to hold his peace until sure of his heart, and he knew that wouldn't happen until he left Wildwood and got his life back in perspective. Sam's sudden realization that he faced several more days of agonizing indecision—long days under Wildwood's spell—depressed him inordinately. How would he be able to resist Libby's charm? he wondered.

She stirred into his embrace then, snuggling closer, throwing an arm over his waist. Sam tensed as his body responded to the scent and softness of her. He cherished the sensation of waking to find Libby so loveably close. He wondered how it would feel to wake this way every morning for the rest of his life. His resistance wavered alarmingly.

I've got to get away from here, he decided for the umpteenth time. *I've got to.*

But how? he wondered. His car was supposed to be ready today, but he couldn't drive it since the doctor had said—

At once, relief washed over Sam. *The doctor.* Of course. Pierce and Gina were heading home to Memphis today. All Sam had to do was hitch a ride. He would return to his house, to his job, to his solitary existence. He would get his life back on an even keel and take a good, long look at it. If he found he couldn't survive without Libby, he would come back for her, throw his whole heart into the romantic seduction for which a woman such as she naturally longed. They would promise each other forever and maybe, just maybe, actually deliver it.

On the other hand, if he found this whole weekend to be a sensual and emotional illusion—and Sam realistically expected to do just that—he would get on with his life...alone. Libby would do the same, and she would do it with a whole heart because he'd kept his cool, never uttering the foolish vows no mortal man could keep.

God, but he was going to miss her.

Chapter Ten

Libby woke minutes later. Her eyes found Sam's instantly, and she smiled at him, raising her head to touch her lips to his.

Oddly unresponsive to that kiss, Sam mumbled a husky, "Good morning."

"Good morning to you, too," she said, attributing his coolness to the lines of weariness etching his handsome face. She eased out of his arms to sit up. "How do you feel?"

"Pretty good, actually," he replied with a shrug, "and hungry enough to eat a horse."

"Would a pig and a chicken do instead?" she asked, swinging her feet to the floor. "I have bacon, eggs—"

"Mmm," he interjected appreciatively. He gave her a boyish grin that did astonishing things to her pulse rate. "Do you mind?"

"Of course not," she said, resisting the urge to stretch beside him and get a head start on the lifetime of loving that lay ahead. Ruthlessly, she reminded herself that he was a sick man—a *starving* sick man. Romance was probably the last thing on his mind this morning. "Coming right up."

She headed first for the bathroom, snatching clean clothes en route, and emerged dressed respectably in corduroy pants and a cotton sweater. Seconds later found her in the kitchen, piling breakfast food onto the counter. Libby hummed as she worked, relishing this opportunity to do something for the man she loved to distraction.

"Mind if I use your phone?" Sam called to her.

"Go ahead," she called back, smiling at his impatience to get in contact with his office or, since it was still so early, maybe his sister. She heard the low murmur of Sam's voice as he talked to someone, heard him raise that voice in what almost sounded like one side of an argument. Frowning, Libby leaned back slightly so she could see him through the open kitchen door, but he'd turned so that he lay with his broad back to her.

Fetch, no doubt smelling the frying bacon, bounded off the bed and into the kitchen. As with every other day, he greeted Libby with a sloppy good-morning kiss when she dropped to one knee to hug him. Chuckling, she pushed him away.

"Are you hungry, too?" she asked.

The canine barked his enthusiastic reply. Libby handed him a dog biscuit from a box in the pantry, the last step in their morning ritual.

"Now scoot. It won't be ready for another ten minutes or so."

Fetch obeyed her command, returning to the bed to land on its occupant with all fours. Sam, who'd now hung up the phone, groaned in response and put his hands to his head, an action that reminded Libby he probably needed another dose of his medicine. She filled a glass with water and walked back into the bedroom to sit on the mattress next to him.

"Time for your tablets," she said, retrieving two of them off the bedside table.

"Thanks." Raising up off the pillow slightly, Sam swallowed the pills and most of the water. Then he handed the glass back to her.

"Bacon will be ready soon," Libby said. "How do you like your eggs?"

"Sunny-side up," he told her.

"Sunny-side up," she mused thoughtfully, reaching out to trace his whisker-stubbled chin with her fingertip. "That just about describes my mood today, and I owe it all to you."

Sam tensed noticeably. "What do you mean?"

Libby gave him a shy smile, searching for the words that might do justice to the happiness inside her. "I'm so glad you're not leaving today, Sam. I feel like I've been given a reprieve on a life sentence of loneliness."

Sam caught his breath. "Look, Libby. I—"

"Anyone home?"

Both Libby and Sam started at the sound of Pierce's call and the loud knock that followed it. Libby jumped to her feet, hurrying to open the door.

"Good morning, Doc," she said, stepping aside so he could enter the room. "Come to check up on our patient?"

"Yeah, and to see if I can't talk him out of going home today."

Libby froze, blurting a startled, "What!" as Pierce made his way past her and over to the bed.

"You look like hell," the doctor told his patient. "And you're going to look worse after a three-hour drive to Memphis."

"Three-hour drive? What's going on?" Libby demanded, catching Pierce's sleeve.

He half turned her way, then looked back at Sam when the lawyer responded. "I've got to go. I can't afford to miss a week of work."

"You're going home today?" Libby exploded, whirling to confront her boss.

Sam blanched and nodded. "Pierce and Gina are giving me a ride."

"But—"

"But nothing," Sam snapped, cutting off her argument. "I have responsibilities, Libby. I can't –Is that your bacon burning?"

With a cry of remembrance, Libby dashed to the kitchen and the smoking skillet. Muttering a heartfelt curse, she moved it to another burner and turned off the flame. She stared at the blackened strips without seeing them, her thoughts in turmoil, her heart breaking. Why was he leaving? she agonized. Last night he'd as good as promised her forever. What had happened?

Maybe he was just hurrying home so he could hurry back, she thought, grasping at nonexistent straws even though she knew that wasn't the case. He'd been less than loving from the moment they rose that morning. Something was terribly amiss.

Libby turned slowly and headed back to her boss, now sitting up on the side of the bed. She watched while Pierce did a quick exam, listened in numb silence when he okayed his patient for travel. Moments later, Pierce nodded his goodbye and left.

Sam's gaze found Libby's across the room. "I'll need my things out of my cabin. Would you . . . ?" His voice faded into nothingness. He searched her troubled face, sighed and patted the bed next to him. "Come here. We need to talk."

Dead certain she was not going to enjoy this conversation, Libby reluctantly joined him.

"I'm sorry I didn't get to tell you I was leaving before he got here." Sam said. "I intended to—just didn't get a chance."

"Why are you doing this?" Libby asked. "You're sick, for heaven's sake. Can't your partners handle your cases for a few days?"

"Probably," he admitted. "But I still have to get away, and the sooner the better . . . for both of us." He frowned at her confusion. "Why are you looking at me like that? I told you my reasons and thought you understood them. Nothing's changed."

"But last night you said . . ." She faltered, suddenly realizing there was a very good possibility he had no memory of his vow of love. Or maybe he did and wanted to forget it in the clear light of day.

"What did I say?" Sam demanded, grasping her arm tightly.

"Never mind," she murmured uneasily, twisting free to stand up. She moved toward the kitchen.

Sam grabbed the back pocket of her pants, halting her progress. *"What did I say?"*

Libby turned to look into his cold blue eyes. "You didn't say a thing. Now I need to know what you're going to do about your car. Want me to call George for you?"

He hesitated, intently studying her expression, and then released her. "I guess you'd better. Tell him I'll pick it up or have someone else do it as soon as possible."

Someone else . . . Recognizing that cop-out for what it surely was, Libby couldn't help but wonder if she would ever see him again. Her heart ached with regret. Her eyes burned with unshed tears that pride wouldn't allow to fall.

"I'll tell him," she mumbled, escaping to the kitchen.

Their oh-so-casual goodbye an hour later haunted Sam all the way down the mountain. Over and over he assured himself that he'd done the right thing. Over and over, he opened his mouth to ask his new friends to turn back. But he didn't speak, and the miles stretched until practicality forbade such a request.

Setting himself more comfortably on the pillow he'd borrowed, Sam stretched out as best he could on the back seat of the doctor's luxury sedan. He closed his eyes, half of his mind back at Wildwood, half of it in the car, now speeding toward home.

Home. Where exactly was home? he wondered, trying to remember the last time he'd really felt as though he belonged. Not since his move to Memphis, he realized, or anytime during his marriage or even the college years before that. Looking back, he decided he'd probably been happiest as a teenager, camping alone on the very mountain he'd just escaped. Or maybe the last couple of days, sharing that same beloved mountain with Libby, a woman who appreciated its splendor as much as he did.

Lost in memories of the rare moments when he'd been at one with nature and at peace with his soul, Sam barely heard the car radio playing until the words of a familiar song burst into his abstraction. He smiled with pleasure and relaxed, letting the romantic lyrics of a song about his beloved Arkansas wash over him—lyrics about falling in love and staying that way forever. Though he suspected the singer referred to the state about which the song had been written, Sam easily applied those loving phrases to Libby, a woman who'd changed his life forever and who just might love him, if he found it in his heart to love her back.

Lord, but he wanted to. He just didn't know if he could.

Libby thought Monday would never end. She worked perfunctorily—posting accounts, paying bills, greeting guests. When quitting time rolled around at five, she kept at it a couple of hours longer, unwilling to return to her apartment and the rumpled bed that would only remind her of what she had lost.

At seven-thirty, Libby finally dragged her weary bones out of the office and down the hallway, followed by Fetch, who'd stuck to her heels all day. Suspecting he sensed her disquiet, Libby sank down on her couch and patted the adjoining cushion. Fetch accepted her invitation, leaping up to sit by her. Ducking that ever-ready tongue of his, Libby scratched behind his ears.

"Sam's been home for—" she glanced at her watch "—eight or nine hours now. He's probably sitting in his favorite chair, watching television or maybe he's in bed...." Libby groaned. She *would* think of that. And what was *he* thinking of? she wondered. Had Libby Turner crossed his mind at all that day? Or was it out of sight, out of life?

Would she ever see him again? Hear from him?

The ring of the phone startled both Libby and her pet. Hand on her hammering heart, Libby lunged for the jangling instrument.

"Hello," she exclaimed, breathless with anticipation.

"Hi," Ramona's disgustingly cheerful voice came back at her. "What on earth have you been doing? Aerobics?"

Heart now sinking back into its usual steady-paced thump, Libby plopped down on the bed and fell over on her side. "No, I ran to catch the phone."

"Expecting an important call, are we?"

Not in the mood for the blonde's highjinks tonight, Libby changed the subject. "How's Ramona?"

Ramona laughed. "She's fine, which is more than I can say for her brother. What on earth did you do to him?"

Libby's heart stopped this time. "What do you mean?" she demanded eagerly, sitting back up.

"Sam told me about his decision to expand Wildwood. He—"

"*Expand?*" Libby blurted, floored. "What on earth are you talking about?"

"He didn't tell you?"

"No."

"He's going to build ten more units, and he wants you to be in charge of *everything* from blueprints to decorating." Ramona laughed with delight. "Isn't that a hoot?"

Libby, stunned to her toenails, had no response.

"Are you still there?" Ramona demanded impatiently.

"Y-yes."

"So what do you think?"

"I, uh . . ." Again words failed Libby, who couldn't help but hope this expansion idea might be Sam's way of keeping their lives linked. Or was it a consolation prize?

"What's wrong with you?" Ramona then exclaimed. "This is *job security*, my friend. Why, a project this size will take months to complete."

"Right," Libby murmured dully.

"I thought you'd be thrilled," Ramona grumbled. "But you're as gloomy as Sam."

"Sam's gloomy?" Libby quickly interjected.

"He'd have to cheer up to get miserable."

"Well, he *is* sick," Libby reminded her, in hopes Ramona would reveal more of her brother's emotional state.

"Yeah, but I really don't think that has anything to do with it." Ramona sighed. "I can't imagine what's wrong with him unless he's worried about his Jag. He does love that car."

"Does he? I didn't pick up on that at all," Libby replied adding, "In fact, that seemed to be the least of his worries...." She lost that thought in the rush of an idea—a wonderful, daring idea that sprang from the romantic heart of her. "Do you think it would help if I drove his car to Memphis tomorrow? It's ready, you know, and I'd love to see you—" *Not to mention your brother.*

"Great idea!" Ramona exclaimed. "We could go shopping, take in a movie, eat dinner at Justine's, you could even spend the night...." Her list faded into silence. "But how are you going to get back home?"

"I'll fly," Libby told her. "It won't cost much, and if it will help Sam—"

"Oh, it'll help all right." Ramona interrupted, adding, "Tell me what you think of my brother after spending a weekend with him."

"He's, um..." Libby hesitated, rejecting choices such as virile, sexy, and irresistible. "Actually, I like your brother."

"Apparently he likes you, too," Ramona responded dryly. "Now let me give you directions to his house. I'll meet you there at, say, noon? That'll give you plenty of time to..."

Libby let Ramona's verbal map wash over her, her thoughts already jumping ahead to the words she intended to say to her handsome boss once she saw him again.

I love you; I want you; I need you, should do for starters she decided. And then she would show that stubborn, frightened man just how much. When she finished with Sam Knight, he would know his heart. More importantly, he would know hers.

Together, they would challenge and conquer his fears about marriage and divorce. Together they would erase the last, faded images of her fantasy knight and, with him, every excuse not to risk her own hesitant heart. Together they would find the happy ending for which they'd both searched a lifetime.

Libby arrived in Memphis way too early on Tuesday, probably because she'd risen before the sun that morning. The Jaguar was a dream to drive. Unfortunately, the crumpled right front fender somewhat spoiled the sleek lines of the powerful car.

Following the directions Ramona had given her, Libby drove directly to Sam's house, a neat brick structure in what looked to be a fairly nice suburb of Memphis proper. At ten on the dot, she pulled into Sam's drive, figuring she would make good use of the extra time, hopefully to talk with and win him before Ramona's arrival.

Libby climbed out of the car, stomping her feet to get the circulation going again after the long drive. She brushed at the creases in her cream-colored pants and the silky black shell under it, then reached back into the vehicle to retrieve the linen blazer, carefully folded over the passenger seat. Nervously, she checked her reflection in the polished black exterior of the car, immediately grimacing and smoothing back the ever-present tendrils of hair that had escaped her French braid.

Giving that up with a snort of irritation, Libby retrieved her purse to head up the concrete walk to Sam's front door. Her gold earrings swayed against her neck as she walked, a sensation she usually relished, but now barely noticed. The butterflies in her stomach had taken sudden flight, swarming upward to flutter past her heart and lodge in her throat.

Libby reached the porch and raised a hand to knock, only to lower it again. Second thoughts assailed her—serious second thoughts. Sam had left *her* after all and gone to incredible lengths to do so. Did she have the right to chase him now?

The door opened. A tall, black-haired woman, no doubt the housekeeper, peered out at her.

"Hi," Libby said, quite intimidated by the woman's elegant demeanor. She wondered fleetingly how Sam survived in a household run by such a forbidding personage. "I'm Elizabeth Turner. I came by to see Sam."

"He's not here."

Libby's jaw dropped. "But, he's got to be," she blurted in disbelief. "He's sick."

"You know it and I know it, but he doesn't," the woman said coldly, folding her arms over her chest.

"But where did he go?" Libby persisted, still not believing her ears.

There was a moment's hesitation while suspicious brown eyes swept Libby from head to toe and back again. "To his office."

Libby gasped. "That idiot!"

A rich chuckle greeted that spontaneous opinion, and the accompanying smile transformed the housekeeper into a human being Libby could easily love.

"What'd you say your name was?" the older woman asked, frowning thoughtfully.

"Elizabeth Turner."

Those brown eyes now began to twinkle mischievously. "Otherwise known as Libby?"

"Yes," Libby told her with a quick nod.

That wonderful smile grew even wider. "My name's Ava Morrison. I'm Sam's housekeeper. We weren't expecting you until noon."

"I got away earlier than I expected."

"Well, I'm sure glad you did. That boy's been a basket case ever since Ramona told him you were coming."

Libby grinned with delight at that loving description of the man she wanted to marry. "He has?"

"Sure has, and now I see why. Would you like to come in and wait for him?"

"I don't know what to do," Libby admitted, glancing back with uncertainty toward the car. "I really need to talk to him, and I may lose my nerve if I have to wait another two hours to do it."

Soft laughter greeted her candid admission. "Does that mean Sam's not the only basket case around here?"

Libby sighed and nodded.

"That's wonderful. Just wonderful." Now beaming, Ava stepped out onto the porch and pointed up the street. "If you stay on this street until you get to the light and then take a right onto Jupiter Road, his office will be six blocks farther down on the left. It's a red brick building, number 101."

"Thanks," Libby murmured, without moving from the porch. She drew in a deep breath and swallowed hard, then laughed nervously. "Gosh, I hope I'm doing the right thing."

"What, exactly, *are* you doing?" Ava asked, eyes sparkling with open curiosity.

Libby hesitated, then impulsively opened up to this woman she had just met, but felt as if she'd known for years. "Throwing myself at the man I love?"

"Hot damn!" Ava exclaimed, suddenly reaching out to embrace her.

As startled by the unexpected expletive as the hug, Libby had no reply. Ava set the younger woman back on her feet and released her.

"Now you get in that car and go see that young man of yours. A visit from you will do more for him than any of that medicine I've been poking down his throat."

"Think so?"

"Know so. Do it."

Libby did, arriving at Sam's office in less than ten minutes. Once again her nerves got the best of her. She scanned the two-story building uneasily, noting the colonial style of the architecture that reminded her just a little of the stately county courthouse back home.

She got out of the car, straightening her apparel and hair as before, and made her way slowly up the wide walkway to the porch. Squaring her shoulders, she reached for the glass door, pushed it open and stepped into a large reception-waiting area.

Anxiously her gaze swept the empty room. Libby saw a low counter, behind which sat two desks and a computer terminal. To her right were three closed doors, to her left two more and an opening that appeared to be the entrance to a hallway. All doors had words painted on them in bold, black letters, but not one said Knight.

Libby frowned and then brightened when she heard voices. Turning toward the sound, she made her way to the hall and peered down it. At the end of the long corridor, she saw an open door and, through it, chairs and one end of what looked to be a conference table.

It sounded like a meeting might be in progress, and since Libby had no intention of butting into one of those, she decided to return to the reception area.

"Well look at you!" a very familiar female voice exclaimed as Libby turned.

"Hi, Ramona," Libby said, smiling in response to the cheerful greeting.

The blonde set down the heavily-laden tray she held and rushed over to give Libby an enthusiastic hug. "You're early. Did Ava send you over?"

Libby nodded and released her. "What on earth is Sam doing here? He's supposed to be home in bed."

Ramona rolled her eyes. "That man called me at the crack of dawn and *demanded* that I come by and drive him to work."

"He's better then?"

"He can walk, if that's what you're asking, but is definitely green around the gills. Nothing Ava or I said could talk him out of coming to work, though, and when we got here—at eight o'clock, mind you—I had to phone all three of his partners and drag them in, too."

"Whatever for?" Libby demanded. "What's going on?"

"Heck if I know. They've been behind closed doors all morning. I finally stuck my head in at ten and called a timeout. Ray, one of the attorneys here, had a call from school. He had to go pick up a sick kid—his wife's car is in the shop. I'm taking advantage of the break to share my coffee. They're bound to need a little sustenance by now." Ramona walked to the counter and picked up the tray again. "Speaking of which, I'd better get this in to them."

"Want some help?" Libby asked, eyeing the full coffeepot, cups, sugar, creamer and bakery sack that Ramona balanced on the tiny tray.

"Would you carry the donuts? I can handle everything else."

"Sure." Libby retrieved the sack.

Ramona smiled her thanks and turned toward the hall. "Follow me."

"I don't want to disturb Sam," Libby cautioned.

"It's okay," Ramona airily assured her. "They're not working at the moment and it might help his morale to know he's got his car back."

Together the women walked down the hall, passing, Libby noted with interest, a closed door with Sam's name on it. As the two of them neared the conference room, Libby's steps began to falter. At the entrance to it, she stopped altogether and placed the sack back on Ramona's tray.

"You're not coming in?" Ramona asked, clearly puzzled by the action.

Suddenly assailed with uncertainty, Libby shook her head. "I think I'll just wait for you two at Sam's house after all."

To Libby's relief, Ramona didn't press it, instead perusing her old friend's face. She smiled at what she saw there. "Want to take a peek at him before you go?"

The brunette nodded eagerly. Ramona stepped through the door, clearing the way for that peek. Libby stuck her head inside the room, immediately spotting the man she adored sitting at the head of the oak conference table, his eyes glued to the top folder of a large stack in front of him.

Though pale and decidedly rumpled looking with his finger-combed hair and loosened tie, Sam still looked good enough to risk a forever after on. Her heart swelled with love for him.

"Say hello," Ramona softly urged leaning forward. "It just might make his day."

Impulsively, Libby stepped into the room. Unnoticed by Sam, still lost in his work, she made her way past the partner standing by the window and the one sitting at the conference table reading the newspaper.

Quietly she eased up on Sam, stopping inches from him to bend down and whisper a husky, "Hi, handsome," right in his ear.

He jumped and then leaped to his feet, engulfing her in an embrace that nearly toppled them both. His mouth found and covered Libby's with a hunger that matched hers and erased all doubts and fears. She wrapped her arms around his neck, molding her body to his, wholeheartedly returning that kiss.

A feminine squeal of delight broke them apart a second later. Rudely aware of the real world—and its smiling occupants—again Libby and Sam separated, both flushed with embarrassment and maybe something more.

Knees suddenly weak, head spinning, Sam plopped back down in his chair to keep from falling. His gaze swept the room, taking note of Ramona's smug smile and the astonished looks on the faces of his partners. Then his gaze fell on Libby, wide-eyed and blushing attractively. She looked as unsteady as he felt, and he wasn't at all surprised when she pulled out a chair and moved to sit in it. Without hesitation, he reached out, tugging her onto his lap instead.

"Meeting's adjourned!" he announced, slapping the flattened palm of his free hand down firmly on the conference table. His eyes never left those of the woman he loved with all his heart, without a doubt, for now and forever.

His partners, taking Sam's not-so-subtle hint, left the room immediately. Ramona, however, wasn't quite as cooperative.

"What's the meaning of this?" she demanded, as any dutiful younger sister should. The corners of her mouth twitched with suppressed laughter.

"I'll tell you later," Sam mumbled, dipping his head to taste his lady love's lips again. Libby opened her mouth to his kiss, and he responded accordingly, deepening the caress until they both gasped for air.

"But I want to know now!" Ramona playfully persisted, clearly pleased with what she saw.

Sam raised his head long enough to mutter, "Beat it and lock the door."

Laughing good-naturedly, Ramona wisely abandoned her teasing and left them alone, locking the door securely behind her.

Sam made good use of the precious privacy, kissing Libby yet again as he began an exploration with his hands that left them both aching with desire.

"I love you," he whispered into the hollow at the base of her throat.

Libby stiffened in his arms and pulled back. She framed his face with her hands, tilting it back so she could read his sincerity. She smiled, a tender expression that brought tears to his eyes. "I love you, too."

"Will you marry me?" he asked.

"You know I will," she replied.

"I do?"

"Yes. I promised that I would never leave you, and in the Turner family that means a wedding."

He frowned, trying to recall such a vow. "You promised me that?"

"Uh-huh," she murmured, raising her face to trail her lips over his chin and cheek. Her fingers moved to his shirt, unbuttoning first one button, another and then another. Sam caught that brazen hand in his so he could think clearly.

"When?"

"Sunday night—or I guess it was really Monday morning—the *first* time you said you loved me." She eased her hand free of his and slipped her fingers into his shirt, teasing his bare chest, which rippled in response.

"What!"

Laughing, Libby kissed Sam and then told him about the nightmare. He shuddered when she finished, suddenly and vividly recalling every frightening detail of the dream, if not their conversation afterward.

"So my subconscious mind knew all along how I felt about you," he mused.

"Apparently," she responded.

He shook his head in wonder. "I understand Ramona's told you about the expansion I've planned for Wildwood."

"She mumbled some such craziness," Libby answered, her words barely distinguishable against the pulse racing in his neck.

"Not craziness," he qualified with a sigh of satisfaction, wrapping his arms more tightly around her. "Sanity. I want as many couples as possible to experience the peace and joy of our resort. I want you to handle everything, just as you did before. I want it to be perfect."

"No can do," she said, much to his astonishment. "I'm moving to Memphis. In fact, I didn't even make a reservation for the flight back home tomorrow."

"Pretty sure of me, were you?" he teased, grinning his delight.

"Pretty sure of *me*," she qualified. "And I wasn't going to leave until I'd convinced you that we had a chance together."

"Let me go on record as saying I'm convinced, and have been since yesterday morning. I knew I'd made a mistake ten minutes after I left you. I just didn't have the nerve to ask Pierce to drive me back, especially after I'd coerced him into taking me as a passenger in the first place. Then I decided it might be best to just go on home and take care of a little business before I got in too deep with you. I wanted to warn my partners I was leaving so they could find a replacement for me."

Libby tensed in his arms. "What are you talking about?"

He smiled. "You don't have to move to Tennessee, Libby. I'm moving back to Arkansas."

"You are?" She twisted out of his arms and sat up straight to stare at him with wide eyes.

"Yep. I called today's meeting to familiarize my partners with my cases. I'm leaving here as soon as I can, and I'm going to take some time off to supervise the building of our house on the back forty of my land there at Wildwood. I figure I can open up an office in Morrilton, build up a clientele there."

Libby nodded thoughtfully. "I suppose that area has its share of marital problems, just like the rest of the world."

"Oh, I'm not going to handle divorces anymore," Sam quickly interjected.

"You're not?"

"Nope. I'm changing the focus of my practice entirely."

"Oh, Sam, that's wonderful," Libby exclaimed, rewarding that decision with a long kiss he felt clear to the marrow.

When she raised her head again, starry-eyed and glowing, he caught his breath with love for her. "Where do you want to honeymoon?" he asked, his thoughts naturally leaping ahead to *that*. "Hawaii? Jamaica? The Riviera?"

"None of the above," Libby replied. "There's only one place to begin our life together."

"Wildwood?" he softly asked.

"Wildwood," she huskily confirmed before their lips met again.

Epilogue

Sam stood by the open window, peering out through the louvered shutters at the beauty that was Wildwood by night. He saw a midnight sky—moonlit and star sprinkled—tall pines, a shimmering lake. He breathed deeply of the April-scented breeze.

Contentment embraced him, caressing his soul, warming his heart. He thought of the past six months—busy months—and of the miracle love had worked on his lonely life. His eyes filled with the tears he'd barely managed to hold at bay during his wedding in the chapel of Wildwood only hours before.

He glanced toward the bed and Libby, sleeping so peacefully there, bathed in the moon's glow streaming through the skylight. He smiled to himself, unashamedly shedding some of those happy tears. How he loved his new wife. What marvelous plans he had for them—plans involving their new house, children, an eternity of togetherness.

Sam looked back out the window, spotting the lighted sign identical to the one that had, one rainy night not so very long ago, challenged the miserable man he once was. *Find Romance At Wildwood.*

He smiled, thinking he was going to have to change that sign to read *Find romance, love and forever after at Wildwood.* That was certainly what he had found.

Suddenly arms slipped around his waist from behind, hugging him. He turned in Libby's embrace, holding her tightly.

She raised her face for his kiss and then pulled back, frowning as she reached up to wipe away his tears.

"Regrets?" she whispered.

"None," he replied with a tender smile. "None at all." Then he scooped Libby up into his arms, carrying her back to their bed so he could prove just that.

At long last, the books you've been waiting for by one of America's top romance authors!

DIANA PALMER

DUETS

Ten years ago Diana Palmer published her very first romances. Powerful and dramatic, these gripping tales of love are everything you have come to expect from Diana Palmer.

In March, some of these titles will be available again in **DIANA PALMER DUETS**—a special three-book collection. Each book will have two wonderful stories plus an introduction by the author. You won't want to miss them!

Book 1
SWEET ENEMY
LOVE ON TRIAL

Book 2
STORM OVER THE LAKE
TO LOVE AND CHERISH

Book 3
IF WINTER COMES
NOW AND FOREVER

 *Silhouette Books*®

DP-1